THIS IS THE KIND OF THING YOU DREAM ABOUT. THE GREAT BATTLES YOU MISSED BECAUSE YOU WERE BORN AT THE WRONG TIME...

As he reached for the cloth covering the easel, Millsaps said, "If you all would move a little closer, please, we'll get on with the briefing. Please everyone, move up." He waited until they were clustered in front of him, away from the walls and in the center of the hut.

He whipped the cloth away so that everyone could see the three-dimensional drawing of the old fort. Millsaps nodded approvingly at the startled reactions of the mercenaries. He said, "There is no mistake. The legend you see on the top is correct. This is our target." As he spoke, he put the tip of the pointer under the title.

It said, simply, *The Alamo. 1836.*

KEVIN RANDLE AND ROBERT CORNETT

REMEMBER THE ALAMO!

CHARTER BOOKS, NEW YORK

This Charter book
contains the complete text of the
original edition. It has been
completely reset in a typeface designed
for easy reading, and was printed from
new film.

REMEMBER THE ALAMO!

A Charter Book/published by arrangement with
the authors

PRINTING HISTORY
TA Publications edition published 1980
Charter edition/July 1986

ISBN: 0-441-71325-4

Charter Books are published by
The Berkley Publishing Group,
200 Madison Avenue, New York, New York 10016.

PRINTED IN THE UNITED STATES OF AMERICA

To T. R. B. Tucker and the thirty-three

HISTORICAL PERSPECTIVE:

   The Battle of the Alamo was fought from
February 23 through March 6, 1836, in the town of San
Antonio de Bexar, in the Territory of Texas, Republic of
Mexico. Lieutenant Colonel William Barret Travis, with
a rag-tag force of one-hundred eighty-three fellow
countrymen, Texans, Mexicans, and volunteers, held off
Generalissimo Antonio Lopez de Santa Anna and his
army of 5,000 crack troops, reputed to be among the
finest fighting men in the world, for thirteen days,
while General Sam Houston and the other leaders of
the Texas Rebellion tried desperately to raise an army,
write a constitution, and form a country. The Texans
won the war but lost the battle.

   One-hundred forty-four years later, the
Second Battle of the Alamo was fought from February
23 through March 6, 1836. With one slight difference—
the presence of an additional force of thirty-three well-
paid mercenaries, hired by a single individual of

enormous cunning, resources, and business sense, who
was totally obsessed with the notion of becoming the
richest man in the world. The impact of this spacio-
temporal event on mainstream HISTORY has yet to be
fully quantified.

Halicar, HISTORIAN
First Assistant to the Chief Archivist

June 12, 1979

Mary Jo Andross
458 Dugdale Drive
Longmont, Colorado 80501

Dr. T.R.B. Tucker
Gonzales Experimental Lab
% Texas-American Oil Company
Gonzales, Texas 78629

Dear Dr. Tucker:

Thank you for the rapid reply to my letter. I am happy that you found my qualifications adequate for your staff.

Nevertheless, I found your questions a little unnerving. I will try to answer them as best I can.

First, we already have two types of time travel. Maybe I should have put that in quotes, since neither type is time travel in the classic sense of the term. Each time we look into the night sky, we are seeing the past. Light, leaving all the stars for Earth, left at least four years ago. Some of it is thousands or even millions of years old. I understand that the Andromeda Galaxy is about two million light years from Earth, so that the light we receive tonight has been traveling for two million years. If we had the power to see individual planets, or events in that galaxy, we would be seeing things as they were two million years ago. And, likewise, if beings in Andromeda could see Earth, they would see a primitive form of man, and not us or our accomplishment. That's not really time travel, but more like peeking into the past.

Second, using Einstein's Theory of Relativity, and the Time Dilation hypothesis, we can travel forward in time. This has already been confirmed by the use of muons in a cyclotron. By accelerating them toward the speed of light, scientists have been able to increase the half-life. By creating a field on Earth similar to that in the cyclotron, we could propel people into the future. Granted, the trip would be slow, and one way; but it is something that we could do with today's technology.

The question that arises from this is whether or not Einstein's theory, that space is curved and a ship traveling through space in a straight line would eventually reach its starting point, is correct. Taking it a step further, time might work the same way and a trip into the future, if taken far enough, would eventually end in the past. The only problem would be calibration of the system.

As I say, I don't understand why you wanted my opinions on time travel, or my theories into it, but there they are. I will be happy to expand on them if you like.

I will be looking forward to your reply. Thank you for your time.

Sincerely yours:

Mary Jo Andross

Mary Jo Andross

July 7, 1979

T.R.B. Tucker
Gonzales Experimental Lab
% Texas-American Oil Company
Gonzales, Texas 78629

Dr. Mary Jo Andross
458 Dugdale Drive
Longmont, Colorado 80501

Dear Dr. Andross:

Please fly down here as soon as you can. We
have plenty of work to do and I believe that you will be
a welcome addition to our staff. Your answers to
the time travel questions prove that. If you had said
that you believe all forms of time travel were
impossible, I would be sending my regrets and we
would still be searching.

Let me know when your plane arrives, and I
will have someone call for you.

Welcome to our staff.

Sincerely yours,

T.R.B. Tucker

ONE

Sage L. Williamson, Chief Scientist for the Texas-American Oil Company, re-read the report from the Gonzales Lab for the fourth time, and still didn't believe it. The report had been on Williamson's desk when he came into work that morning with a cryptic memo from Halvorson, the Director of Research, paper-clipped to the front sheet.

The note said simply, "Sage, you'd better read this. I've seen it and it appears to work. Dave."

Williamson pulled the note from under the paper clip and tossed it toward an "in" basket. The letterhead on the first page of the report proclaimed:

Division of Scientific Research
Office of Applied Theories
Texas-American Oil Company
Substation of the Application
of Temporal Investigation Techniques
Gonzales, Texas

Williamson read the report and then re-read it to make sure that he understood it. It was rather lengthy for a preliminary, being some twenty pages plus a half-dozen appendices, and it dealt with an area of research with which he was unfamiliar. When he finally understood it, he read it a third time just to make sure he had understood it properly. It was then that the full implications of the report finally began to sink home.

What the report detailed, in dry, scientific terminology, was a series of initial operational tests of a piece of apparatus or, more precisely, a system known as an integrated trans-spacio-temporal physical transference system.

Less than an hour after he had finished studying the report, Williamson was standing in the cramped office of the Director of Research, wishing that he had followed company protocol by summoning Halvorson to his office instead. Without waiting for Halvorson to speak, he waved the report at him and said, "Tell me now, Dave, are you absolutely sure of your facts on this thing?"

"As sure as I can be. I don't understand all the theory behind it, sometimes I don't think even Tucker does, but I do grasp the basic operating principles, and when I asked them to set up a demonstration, they did it on the spot, letting me select the event location. There was no time for them to arrange some sort of elaborate hoax, and there's nothing in Tucker's background to suggest that sort of crookedness. Oh, he drinks too much, and smokes too much, and womanizes too much, but he takes this thing of his very seriously.

"Personally, I'm convinced that Tucker can do exactly what he claims he can do."

"Convinced enough to stake your professional reputation on it?"

"Sage, I wouldn't stake my professional reputation on the sun rising tomorrow. I'm as sure as I can be. That's all

I can say. Tucker is dealing with an area on the very fringes of science. We may even have to re-think science as we know it. Professionally, I reserve judgment until further, extensive testing has been done. Personally, I think that Tucker has come up with something that will have old Albert Einstein doing somersaults in his coffin."

At twenty minutes past ten on Thursday morning, the red and white Bell Jet Ranger helicopter settled onto the grassy runway behind the six-strand, barbed wire fence that separated the airstrip from the tarmac highway and landed amid a choking, swirling storm of dust that momentarily obscured the emblem on its side, a white star set in a red block state of Texas, with a red outline silhouette of the United States and superimposed with a black oil well—the corporate logo of the Texas-American Oil Company. Then the turbine whined away into silence, the rotors swung down to a halt, and the rubber door seals plopped open, letting the air-conditioning out and the ninety-plus degree Fahrenheit Texas summer in.

Williamson sagged as the blast furnace breath from outside hit him, instantly soaking his white Arrow shirt with sweat and taking the press out of his powder blue silk tie. Williamson pulled at the knot, loosening it, and unbuttoned his shirt collar. Taking his briefcase with him, he stepped down carefully from the helicopter as the corporate pilot disappeared behind the aircraft to do whatever it is corporate pilots do while corporate big wheels are busy making themselves feel important.

Williamson was piqued to find no welcoming committee waiting to greet him. There wasn't even a guard at the gate, which stood wide open in the high cyclone fence that surrounded the laboratory complex on the other side of the road. In fact, there wasn't much of a laboratory complex.

Just a white, wood frame house, a couple of small corrugated metal sheds, a fenced-off transformer, and one long, low, concrete building painted white. Williamson took the latter to be the lab proper and, crossing the road, passed unchallenged through the gate; he tried the knob on the laboratory door.

It was solidly locked.

Somewhat disgusted by the whole thing, Williamson trudged back up to the house, knocked on the door, got no answer, and knocked again. Still getting no answer, he turned the knob. The door opened easily.

He walked up the two short steps and into a gloomy and incredibly cluttered living room where a bearded young man, in white cut-offs and sandals and wearing a dark blue T-shirt, was sprawled across the sofa busily shuffling papers and scribbling occasional notes in the margins as he checked figures with a Texas-Instruments pocket calculator. The youth had a pair of white stereo headphones clamped to his ears and plugged into a large reel-to-reel tapedeck sitting next to the sofa. He was obviously oblivious to Williamson's presence.

Williamson walked over to the sofa and looked down at the man who continued to ignore his visitor. Williamson glanced at the paper the man was working on but could make no sense of the complex mathematical equations covering it. The man's T-shirt, Williamson observed, stated, "Property of the University of Iowa Athletic Department, IDAHO CITY, OHIO." That made even less sense than the equations.

"Excuse me," said Williamson, a bit louder than necessary, "but could I have a minute of your time?"

The young man pulled the earphones down around his neck and squinted up at Williamson.

"Hello," he said. "Can I help you with something?"

"I was beginning to wonder. My name is Sage Williamson. I'm from the home office in Dallas. I'm here to speak with Mr. Tucker about his . . ."

That was as far as he got. The young man turned his head toward the rear of the house, shouted, "Mary Jo, that guy from Dallas is here to see about the Tucker Transfer," slipped the earphones back on his head, gulped down a large slug of Pickett's beer, and went back to scribbling at his notes.

Williamson stood there for a moment dumbfounded, then shrugged and walked toward what he assumed was the room where "Mary Jo" might be found. As he neared the louvered swinging double door, he nearly collided with a startlingly young brunette who was dressed only in a string bikini and a perfect tan.

The only thing more startling about the young woman than her appearance was her conversation when she opened her mouth. The voice was husky; it could have been sensuous, but the effect was ruined by the rapid-fire chatter of words.

"Hi! I'm Mary Jo Andross. Actually my name is Mariland Josephene, but everyone calls me Mary Jo. That's much better, don't you think? I mean after all, Mariland Josephene is just too long and it sounds awful. That's Bob Cunningham over on the couch. I'm sorry if he wasn't very friendly, but you really have to excuse him. He's simply impossible to talk to when he's working on something important. You must be Mr. Williamson from the home office in Dallas. Tuck told us you were coming out. Excuse me, I've got to close the door. If you leave it open it gets terribly hot in here. The air conditioner really isn't sufficient. We used to have three of them, but Tuck took out the other two and reinstalled them in the lab to keep the equipment cool because some bureaucrat at the home office wouldn't send us the air conditioners we needed for the lab because they hadn't been vouchered properly. I'm sorry. I do hope you weren't the bureaucrat. Would you like a glass of iced tea? Just a minute, I'll get you one."

The girl walked over to the couch, pulled one of the headphones off the young man, whispered something in his ear, and stuck the headphone back in place. He smiled, nodded, and waved at Williamson, then went back to his studies.

"You see? I told you Bob's impossible when he's working on something important. Tuck's down in the lab right now with Andy, that's Andy Kent, recalibrating the trans-spacio-temporal coordinate system's zero ground point indicator on the induction field readout circuit. I'll call down and tell them you're here, but first let me get you that iced tea. Do you take sugar? I hope not. It's bad for your teeth and puts on extra calories. I never use sugar. The kitchen is this way."

Williamson took advantage of the momentary pause to gesture to the couch. "What's he listening to, rock music?"

"Bob? Oh no. He hates rock music. Except I think he listens to Blue Oyster Cult sometimes when he thinks no one else is around to hear, but he claims he only listens to the classics . . ."

The girl never did quiet down, but she did fix him an iced tea without sugar, and she did call down to the laboratory to tell Tucker he had arrived. And somewhere in between that and making small talk with the pilot and getting off on two-hundred tangents that Williamson couldn't follow, she managed to tell him that she had done post-doctoral work in physics at Stanford and at MIT, and that Bob was working on his second PhD after taking his first in mathematics, and that Andy was a whiz of an electrical engineer and knew about all there was to know about computers and that he and Tuck would be up in a minute, and on and on, until Williamson stopped listening to her.

Bewildered, he took his iced tea out into the living room, carefully removed an enormous pile of papers from an overstuffed armchair of indeterminate age and origin, and sat down in it to taste his tea and await Tucker's arrival.

He had no sooner sat down than the door opened and two men came into the living room from outside. One looked about thirty years old, had a small moustache and close-cut hair, and was carrying a can of coke. He was wearing a pair of cut-off army pants and a dark blue T-shirt. The other man looked to be in his late forties or early fifties, though Williamson knew from his file that he was well over sixty. He had thick silver hair through which he constantly ran his fingers whenever not using them to remove the small, plastic-tipped cigar from his mouth to gesture in the air with it. He was wearing a blue and white plaid, long-sleeved shirt with the cuffs rolled up. Williamson recognized him immediately as T.R.B. Tucker.

Dr. T.R.B. Tucker leaned back among the torn and split green vinyl cushions supported by the flaking battleship grey painted steel frame of the swivel chair and lighted a small White Owl cigar with a paper match. He puffed briefly until the end of the cigar glowed, then shook out the match and tossed it in the general direction of the ashtray. The glowing ember described a small orange arc that somehow found its way to the ceramic bowl and avoided igniting the pyramids of paper concealing the desk top.

Tucker gestured expansively with the cigar, enscribing little circles in the air as he patiently went over the tests again with Williamson listening. "The operational trials have been fully documented, of course. We have a recording of a 'lost' speech given by Lincoln before his election, a 16-mm film of the *Titanic* sinking, a valuable seismographic reading of the San Francisco earthquake of 1905, and a set of full-color telephoto slides showing the state-ordered death by crucifixion of one Jesus of Nazareth."

Williamson shook his head slowly as he looked from Tucker, to Bob who had given up the earphones for a few minutes, to Mary Jo who had found an old bathrobe, and then to Andy who was sitting with his eyes closed and his feet on a coffee table. "I can see a certain commercial application of your device, as soon as the authenticity of the photos and tapes can be established, but I fail to see anything truly valuable in your invention."

There was a moment of silence while Tucker puffed. "The historical questions that can be answered should be of great consequence to many."

"I don't mean to sell your work short. Those pictures you showed me are amazing. But viewing the past seems to be more of a novelty than anything else. It will increase our knowledge in an abstract, but a fairly useless, way I'm afraid."

Bob turned on Williamson. "There is no such thing as valueless information. Anything that helps us understand the past will make our future better. All you clowns worry about are profit margins and production quotas, to the detriment of everything and everyone else. I don't know why I even sit here and listen to you." He stood, glanced at Mary Jo and then Andy, and walked out of the room.

When the outside door slammed, Williamson said, "I didn't mean to upset your staff. And I certainly didn't mean to imply that your work was useless. Certainly there are any number of scholarly aspects that could be exploited. I merely meant that, to a corporation whose goal is energy production, your machine has little value."

Mary Jo cut in. "Oh we understand. We expect that kind of thing from your people in Dallas. After all, that's your job, isn't it. Making money for the stockholders. Sometimes, at this end . . ."

"That's enough, Mary Jo. We're getting side-tracked here." Tucker leaned his elbows on his knees and put his chin in his hand. "Your director of research, what's-his-name, seemed impressed with the film we made of Pickett's Charge at the Battle of Gettysburg."

"Yes. Yes. But that's what I mean. More pictures. They don't do us any good at all. You're missing the essence here."

Understanding dawned on Tucker. He sat up and he laughed. "Oh no, Mr. Williamson, I believe you've missed the point. The integrated trans-spacio-temporal physical transference system is more than just a means to seeing into the past and collecting pictures of it. It is, to use the term favored by H. G. Wells and two-hundred other science fiction writers, an 'honest-to-God time machine'."

Williamson jerked upright as if he had been shot. "You don't mean to say that you could, can, send people back, back into the past?"

"But of course. That's why it's called a physical transference system."

"But you haven't sent anyone back, have you?"

"No. Only various types of recording equipment. But we could, given sufficient funding," Tucker smiled. "I suppose you can think of one or two commercial applications now, can't you?"

"Most definitely," Williamson said quietly. "Most definitely."

HISTORICAL PERSPECTIVE

Jim Bowie arrived in San Antonio on January 17, 1836, after the siege that had taken the Alamo away from General Cos and his Mexican force. Bowie's orders, from Sam Houston, were to blow up the fort after he had removed all the supplies that the infant Texas army could use. Bowie planned to do just that, but once he arrived in San Antonio with his tiny force of volunteers, he hesitated. The commander of the Alamo garrison explained that he didn't have the men to man the fort, and Bowie said that he didn't have the manpower to drag away the captured cannons.

Less than three weeks later, William Travis rode into San Antonio with the entire Texas cavalry, about thirty men. Travis wasn't happy with his orders, and he wrote nearly everyone in the command positions of the Texas army but, in the end, Travis had to go to San Antonio. Almost from the moment he rode in, he was in a fight with Bowie.

Colonel Joseph C. Neill, who had inherited

command of the Alamo as the other top officers left, couldn't wait to turn command over to someone else. He wanted to give it to Travis who held a regular commission, but the majority of the men were volunteers and they wanted to elect their own leader. Neill tried to leave Travis in command and sneak out of town, but the plan didn't work, and an election was held. Bowie won by a landslide.

Travis claimed that Bowie's command didn't extend to his men, and Bowie said that it extended over all the troops in the Alamo. At any rate, the suggestion was made that Bowie and Travis set up a co-command, and they agreed. All orders would be endorsed by both officers.

With the matter of command settled, at least temporarily, the men in the Alamo began to prepare for the arrival of the Mexican army. Spies had told them that Santa Anna was moving north. Both Travis and Bowie knew that the Mexicans would come to San Antonio. They had to. They couldn't afford to leave a fairly large force of Texans sitting on their supply lines, and they had to avenge the defeat they had suffered at the Alamo in December, 1835.

Halicar, HISTORIAN
First Assistant to the Chief Archivist

TWO

The Special Assistant to the President of Texas-American, Michael Travis, read over the geologist's report with deliberate care, obvious disgust, and a strong sense of exasperation.

The northern Mexican oil finds were turning out to be bigger than had been previously thought. Enormously so. There was a strong possibility that the total find could exceed all known Middle East reserves. And those damned Mexicans were insisting on developing it all as a national resource, without the help of any gringo Norteamericanos. The United States could buy the Mexican oil at world market prices, just like everyone else, but there would be no preferential sales agreements, and no big multinational corporations, yankees or otherwise, cutting themselves a nice fat chunk of the action off the top.

Travis, already a wealthy man, could not stand to see such opportunities to increase that wealth slip away. He had developed a taste for the finer things early in life, and his job with Texas-American helped him acquire most of them. But the potential for further growth with Texas-American was limited by the corporate structure, the family infighting among the majority stockholders, and nepotism that ran wild. Travis wanted five or ten million dollars in a Swiss account and a few thousand acres of prime cattle range in Argentina.

The Mexican find was going to turn out to be worth several billion dollars and it was unfortunate that Travis' stocks weren't going to benefit from the development.

Travis sighed, put the Mexican file into the "out" basket and picked up the latest report from the Gonzales Lab. He read it carefully, the germ of an idea forming slowly in the back of his mind. By the time there was the soft buzz from his intercom to remind him of his daily meeting with H. Perot Lewis, Travis had thought of a scheme so wild that he couldn't believe that it had any possibility of working, and yet, the Gonzales report suggested that it might. He grabbed the Mexican file and stuffed it and the Gonzales report in the leather folder, the front of which was gold-embossed with the words, "DAILY BRIEFS", and took the private elevator upstairs to his boss's office.

H. Perot Lewis, President and Chairman of the Board of the Texas-American Oil Company, sat in his twenty-second floor office atop the TexAm Building in downtown Dallas, and worried.

He was not particularly worried about business. The company's profits were up nearly six-hundred percent from last year, and the previous year had not been a bad one. Nor was he overly concerned about the upcoming Senate Investigating Committee hearings charged with looking into these increased profits despite alleged national shortages of oil and worldwide energy scarcities. Taking care of such annoying governmental interference was what he paid a team of economic and legal specialists a completely unreasonable annual retainer for.

What worried H. Perot Lewis, as he sat in his suede armchair behind his ebony and marble desk on this crisp April morning, was that he was running out of time.

Born Harold Perot Lewis on Christmas Day, 1929, a name he hated and never used because he felt it unmasculine, H. Perot Lewis was not exactly a self-made man, though few would have argued the point had he cared to claim it.

In 1946 he had inherited a moderately successful but insignificant oil company from his father, Harold Senior. At that time the company had assets totaling a few million dollars. The family fortune, because of a substantial cattle ranching operation, ran slightly less than a million. Under the direction of Harold Junior, Texas-American had become a multi-billion dollar business, and H. Perot Lewis had become one of the twenty richest men in the world.

Which was precisely the problem.

More than anything else, H. Perot Lewis wanted to be the richest man alive. He had decided that at age twenty-six when he had taken over the company. Fortunately, he had the right combination of gambler's luck, intuitive foresight, and killer instinct to have a very good chance of getting the job done.

What he did not have was time.

At 10:00 the day before, Fred Harris had called and had taken it all away from him. Harris, one of Lewis' very few friends, was also his personal physician. During Lewis' last physical, Dr. Harris suspected he had found something which he wished he had not. Now he was rock-bottom sure of it and had called Lewis for further consultation.

Dr. Harris had discovered a tumor. Malignant. Advanced. Inoperable. There could be no doubt. Five of Dallas' most eminent physicians concurred with his diagnosis.

At fifty-one years of age, H. Perot Lewis had no more than six months to live.

Less than six months to obtain his goal, which seemed to be receding faster than the lure of desert water in the eyes of a man dying of thirst.

Lewis swirled the bourbon in his glass, the ice cubes tinkling, as he thumbed through the report that Sage Williamson had brought him earlier that morning. It contained nothing that could be translated into a "now" profit, nothing that could be translated into billions that would achieve the single obsessive goal of becoming the richest man in the world.

It all took time. And Lewis had little left.

For over an hour Lewis and Travis had been sitting in the conference room that connected with Lewis' office, discussing the two reports that seemed, somehow, to be related. Travis pulled the scattered sheets together and straightened the edges by tapping them on the table.

"As I see it," he said, "the Mexican claim to the oil fields is purely historical."

"Yes. And that locks it up for them."

Travis stared at the top sheet of the report from Gonzales. The idea that had bloomed in the elevator on the way up was taking a firmer shape as he sat there listening to Lewis lament the escape of the Mexican oil. He hesitated, not wanting to mention it, hoping that Lewis would say something that would enable him to carefully bring up the subject.

Travis tried another tack. Having studied history in college, he was aware of the development of Mexico and how close some of it had come to being a part of Texas. He said, "It's too bad that the Texas War for Independence didn't take a different turn."

Lewis slammed his bourbon glass to the desk. "Damn it, Mike, if you have something to say, say it. Don't continue to beat around the bush."

"I don't know about this." Travis stood and moved to the windows where he could look out on downtown Dallas. Rain began, streaking the glass. "It would seem to me, by providence we have been presented with, or rather given an opportunity to . . ."

"Get to the point."

Seeing no way around it, he plunged onward. "As I said, the only claim the Mexicans have is historical. With the machine Tucker invented, we have a way to negate that claim."

Lewis was at first surprised and then amused. For the first time in two days, he forgot all his problems as he burst into laughter. "Good, Mike, very funny. Now forget that nonsense. Is there any other business?"

"No sir. That about covers it."

Just over a week later, one of the strangest that Travis had ever lived, he again sat in the conference room. He opened his folder and said, "I believe, sir, that I've found the man for the job if he can be persuaded to take it."

"Who is he?"

Travis flipped the pages, thinking that it was unbelievable that he was sitting here discussing the hiring of a mercenary when only a week ago Lewis had been ridiculing the idea of changing Mexico's historical ownership of the oil. He reached into the folder and brought out an 8 by 10 color glossy print which he pushed across the table.

"His name is Robert Brown, and as you can see here, he

is a former Army lieutenant colonel. I've got a complete report on him," said Travis, handing a thick grey folder to Lewis.

"I'll study that later. Give me the highlights right now."

"Robert Kevin Brown was born on September 10, 1934, in Cedar Rapids, Iowa, the son of a railroad section foreman. Brown enlisted in the Army in 1951, at age seventeen, and fought as an enlisted man during the Korean War, rising to the rank of sergeant first class. After the war he obtained a commission as a second lieutenant through OCS and earned a Bachelor of Science degree in politics and military history from the University of Texas at Austin. He remained in the Army and entered the Vietnam War as a captain, eventually advancing to lieutenant colonel. He's a graduate of the U.S. Army Airborne School, the Infantry Officer's School, Ranger School, and the Special Warfare School. Highly decorated for bravery both as an officer and an enlisted man, he was considered by his superiors to be a brilliant, though at times unorthodox, even eccentric, military commander. He retired from the service after 22 years, on the eve of his promotion to colonel, in protest of what he viewed as the selling out of the South Vietnamese people to the communists. He now lives in Denver, Colorado."

"All right. He's experienced. But can he put together the team we're talking about? Can he take them into the fray and pull off a victory?"

"You've got to remember that he has to be kept ignorant of the true nature of the mission until the last possible instant. I'm convinced that a man like Brown would never undertake the job if he knew the real purpose. Nor would he be swayed with offers of large amounts of money or personal power. There's no telling how all these factors will combine to help or hinder the mission."

"Which doesn't answer the question."

"It's impossible to say whether or not any man could do

it, but if it can be done, then Robert Brown is the man for the job."

Lewis picked up the photo and studied the picture. All he could see was Brown's short blonde hair, the blue-grey eyes that looked almost colorless and the silver oak leaves of a lieutenant colonel. Above the left pocket were several rows of ribbons that attested to Brown's experience.

"So what do we offer this man," asked Lewis, "if he doesn't need money or want power?"

Travis looked up. "We give him a cause worth fighting for."

After three days of talking, arguing, and debating, Robert Brown and H. Perot Lewis had found a course of action that they both liked. For a fee, a rather substantial one, Brown would draw up a plan to be used to capture a fort in a small African dictatorship. For a further fee, he would provide lists of equipment he felt necessary to ensure the success of the plan, and, for an additional fee, he would design a training program for the small cadre that would aid the African rebels.

Although Brown did nothing during the meetings that would indicate anything other than belief in the story told by Lewis and Michael Travis, he hadn't believed the story for more than thirty seconds. That didn't matter. He knew enough about the Republic of Equatorial Guinea to believe that any change in the despotic government, no matter what the reasons for the change, would be for the better.

So, he signed the documents that pledged his assistance to the Texas-American Oil Company, provided Travis with a list of supplies that he would want immediately, and then told him what he wanted in the newspaper ad that would be used to recruit the assault team.

Four days later the ad appeared in a dozen newspapers around the country.

THREE

Jessica G. Thompson stepped out of the bathtub and toweled herself dry. From the kitchen she could hear the voice of the radio announcer.

"Good afternoon. For WFAA News, this is Lee Dennis. It's ninety-three degrees in downtown Dallas and it's sunny out there, perfect bikini weather. In the news: Police fought a four-hour pitched gun battle with five terrorists at Love Field today. A spokesman for the President's Council of Economic Advisors said this morning that consumers can expect food prices to climb another ten percent during the second half of this year. Federal Marshals have seized the Governor's personal records as evidence in the Second Texas Stock Fraud Scandal. And the Tarrant County Girl Scouts begin their annual cookie drive tomorrow. We'll have details in a moment, but first this word from Jax, the Faubacher family brew."

Jessie wrapped herself in a blue terrycloth robe and walked to the refrigerator for her second Coke of the morning. It might be afternoon for WFAA and the city of Dallas, but when you've been up until 4:00 AM, five minutes past noon is not afternoon. At least not *good* afternoon.

She picked up the Dallas Morning News from the table, turned to the classified ads, and ran her fingernail down the Help Wanted column. Since her discharge from the Air Force she had been unable to find any kind of work other than waiting on tables in establishments where the management required her to smile sweetly when some drunken hick from Farmer's Branch pinched her bottom as she brought him his bourbon and water, "Losa ice ya heah." There just didn't seem to be much of a job market for an ex-photo interpreter with a Bachelor's degree in geopolitics from the University of Texas and a couple of rusty medals in an old jewelry box.

She was surprised that she hadn't seen the ad when she first opened the paper because it was in boldface type set off with big black asterisks.

****

WANTED: SECURITY PERSONNEL for overseas employment with major American corporation. Must be experienced in the use and maintenance of firearms, small unit tactics, and perimeter defense. Must be single, physically fit, and apolitical. Combat experience required. Salary commensurate. Send resume to Michael Travis, Texas-American Oil Company, Dallas, Texas. An equal opportunity employer M/F.

****

She re-read the ad carefully. It wasn't the sort of thing that a woman would answer, even if it did say equal opportunity employer, but then, there couldn't be many women who had been awarded the Silver Star and a Purple Heart for leading a group of enlisted clerk-typists to safety when the Viet Cong had overrun Tan Son Nhut Air Base northwest of Saigon.

Even now the memory of that day stood out stark in her mind. The events occurring around her then were wrapped in the grey, swirling mist of confusion that surrounds the action of battle in many soldiers' minds, but her own participation in that awful, terror-filled twenty-four hours held a razor-edge sharpness of clarity that she would never, could never forget.

It had been early morning, and there had been only two other officers in the duty hut. Major Speas, who had the night watch, had not yet left because his relief was late in arriving. Captain Hanover had, like Jessie, come in half an hour early to clear up some paperwork. There were two enlisted men in the outer office, a couple of clerk-typists.

Speas and Hanover were making chit-chat and drinking some of the abomination Speas called coffee, which the major had brewed sometime the night before. Jessie had intelligently, but politely, refused a cup. The air conditioner was whirring away at full blast, but it was already sticky in the office, and the crisp lines of her starched fatigues had wilted during the walk over from her room in the FOQ.

Suddenly the chatter between Speas and Hanover died and, in the brief quiet, Jessie could hear a series of rapid, hollow crumping noises. She did not immediately recognize the sounds as explosions, but the sporadic crackling that followed she identified as gunfire.

Before any of them could move, the door burst open and an Army helicopter pilot, dressed in flight suit and helmet, his .38 caliber service revolver in his hand, ran in shouting. "Charlie's overrunning the field. You people better get the hell to the bunkers. The perimeter didn't hold. We're taking all the aircraft to Nha Be. Binh Hoa and Cu Chi are under attack."

And, having said all that needed to be said, he just as quickly turned and sprinted away.

Unbelievingly, they all sat frozen for a moment, Jessie with her pen still poised over a requisition form for stereoscopic magnifiers, Speas and Hanover with their coffee cups half raised. Then the rising wail of the ground attack siren broke through to them, and they all scrambled for the door.

Speas dropped his china mug and it clattered to the floor. He was the first one outside. Hanover slammed his cup down on the desk top, slopping coffee across the requisition, and followed the major. Because she was sitting behind the desk, and because she turned at the doorway and went back for her purse, Jessie was the last one out of the office, a fact which probably saved her life.

There was a flat splattering noise, like shrimp suddenly dropped into a deep frier, and the windows in the outer office flew inward, changing to a cloud of glass splinters that peppered the interior walls like a thousand crystal darts thrown from the hand of a giant.

Jessie threw herself to the floor and dug furiously in the purse for her revolver, a nickle-plated, five-shot .38 special with a snub-nosed barrel. A gift from her father just before she left for Vietnam, it was an unauthorized, unapproved weapon, and Jessie had been very careful not to show or tell anyone about it until now, but just at that moment, the fact that she wasn't supposed to have it seemed rather unimportant.

Both the clerk-typists, a couple of scared teenagers, had still been in the outer office. Maybe they were waiting for the officers to tell them what to do. They were noncombatants, and this was Saigon. People weren't supposed to be trying to kill them. That was something that happened only to the grunts out in the field.

Jessie heard one of them moan from behind a desk but she was momentarily too stunned to see what was wrong with the man. There was a ragged row of holes running across the front wall that stopped and started again when it encountered a window or the doorway, and just beyond the front step, Jessie could see both Major Speas and Captain Hanover lying on the ground. They were very still, and Hanover's leg seemed to be bent at a curious, twisted angle.

Jessie found the revolver, snapped open the cylinder so she could check the loads, and pushed it shut again. She looked up just in time to see a Vietnamese put his right sandal on the front step. He was wearing black pajamas and had an AK-47 assault rifle in his hands. Jessie didn't hesitate. She steadied the revolver in both hands and pulled the trigger. She kept pulling it until the hammer clicked twice on empty chambers. The Viet Cong collapsed a foot in front of her outstretched arms, his head in a straight line with the barrel of the snub-nose. Jessie struck the man twice on the temple with the heel of the pistol's grip, and kicked the rifle across the floor in the direction of one of the enlisted men.

Jessie Thompson, the freckle-faced little girl from Denton, Texas, who had hunted jackrabbits and deer with her dad when she was twelve years old, had just killed her first human being. And she wasn't sickened or disgusted or ashamed, just scared, and awfully glad that it wasn't her lying on the floor dead.

"Uh, nice shooting, Lieutenant," said the airman.

Jessie glanced at him and then nodded toward the far corner behind the desk. The airman shook his head.

"Rogers is dead, I think."

"You think?"

The airman swallowed and nodded emphatically.

Jessie scrambled over to the corner and looked behind the desk. Airman First Class Rogers was dead all right. A bullet had entered his right temple and exited the left side of the back of his skull.

Jessie did feel sick then. The Viet Cong she'd killed was a stranger, but Billy Rogers was someone she knew, someone she'd worked with for three months, someone who had a girl back home waiting for a marriage that would never take place. Jessie became aware that Airman Meyer was trying to talk to her.

"Lieutenant? Lieutenant?"

"Yes, what is it?"

"What do we do now?"

"What did you say?"

"I said what do we do now? We can't stay here. Charlie's going to be all over this place in a couple of minutes."

The shock of the rapidity of events began to melt away as Jessie thought hard for a moment. "I guess we'd better try to make it to the bunkers over by Hotel Three. Do you know how to use that thing?" she asked, pointing to the AK-47.

"I've never used one before," answered Meyer, "but give me half a minute and I think I can figure it out."

"Take fifteen seconds. Charlie already found us here once. I don't think we want to hang around and give him a second chance."

Speas and Hanover were dead. There had been little doubt in Jessie's mind that they were when she first saw them lying beyond the front step. She had forced herself to check, to make sure, and then went on. There would be enough time for crying later. Now there was only time to worry about staying alive.

The firing was becoming widespread. Everywhere about

them they could hear the crackling of M-16's, the rattle of AK's, the deep-throated hammering of M-60 machine guns, punctuated at irregular intervals by the pop of .38 caliber revolvers and the explosions of grenades. They worked their way slowly between the buildings, staying low, using garbage cans and trash dumpsters for cover, pressing in close to the walls of the quonset huts and frame buildings. Not far from the Mess Hall they nearly got shot by three cooks who were startled when Meyer loosed a long burst from the AK at a group of five Viet Cong running across the field, dropping two of them.

The cooks were hiding under a picnic table set near the back door of the mess hall, and when Meyer fired the AK from behind them, they rolled over and lined up their rifles, but seeing a woman, didn't shoot. The cooks were still dressed in their white uniforms, though they were covered with dirt from hiding under the picnic tables. Incongruously, one of them wore a helmet with a camouflage cover. They were armed, respectively, with an M-16, an M-1 carbine, and a butcher knife. Not one of them was more than nineteen years old.

"Goddammit, Lieutenant, you two could have got shot doing that, ah, ma'am," said one of them.

"And we all could get shot standing here talking about it. We're going to try to make the bunkers over by the helipads. Come if you want. There isn't time to stand here arguing."

An RPG exploded somewhere nearby. It was enough to make up the cooks' minds for them.

They kept working their way toward the bunkers and picking up stragglers along the way including two more administrative specialists without weapons; an Air Policeman who gave up his revolver to one of the paper shufflers and later his M-16 when he gave up his life to a stray bullet; a motor-pool mechanic with an M-3 submachine gun. And when they came across the less fortunate, they picked up their weapons and ammunition without regard to nationality.

Near the PX they found an MP sergeant sitting in a corner of packing crates, his broken left arm, smashed by an AK round, hanging useless at his side, his right arm extended, hand gripping a .45 semi-automatic pistol which roared rapidly as he knocked down VC like tenpins. They gave him a hand, and he gave them his rifle.

They worked their way along "The World's Largest PX" until they were within sight of the helipad, but couldn't make it to the bunkers. The fighting in the area was too intense, so they fell back to one of the concrete administrative buildings, which offered at least some protection, and deployed inside.

They repelled a brief attack by about a dozen Viet Cong late in the morning and in mid-afternoon rescued seven enlisted men from a nearby building that was under machine gun and RPG fire. They did it by assaulting the enemy-held building from two different directions. The MP sergeant, left arm bandaged and splinted, led one group. Jessie led the other.

They advanced undetected as far as possible and then leapfrogged ahead by fire and movement. A group of inexperienced, noncombatant teenagers, led by a twenty-year-old sergeant with a shattered arm and a girl officer, bombed the enemy out of existence with captured hand grenades made in China.

It was during this attack that Jessica Thompson killed three more men with a revolver she wasn't supposed to have, one of them by beating him in the throat with an empty gun, and blew up a machine-gun emplacement. And she did it all while hobbling about with a bullet in her right leg that later left an ugly red scar across her inner thigh.

They returned to the concrete block building with the

seven rescued airmen, an RPD machine gun, an RPG 7 with a half-dozen rocket-propelled grenades, and a motley collection of AK's, SKS carbines, and American-made arms. They held off two attacks during the night, the second of which degenerated into hand-to-hand fighting because they were so low on ammunition, and during which "a one-legged lady lieutenant," as the MP sergeant would later refer to her, "shot three Charlies with a captured AK and killed one more with a dead cook's butcher knife."

When help arrived the next morning, as the last of the Viet Cong who had launched the Tet Offensive were being mopped up, there were looks of stunned disbelief and then a ragged cheer from the rescuers when a group of dirty, bloody kids, dressed in khaki and blue and green and white cook's uniforms, carried a half-conscious "lady lieutenant," who still clutched a nickle-plated, snub-nosed revolver in one hand and a butcher knife in the other, on their shoulders through the bullet-pocked door and into the sunshine.

During the fight, no one had questioned Jessie's right or ability to command. She was the only officer present, and it had been natural for her to take charge. And once an officer takes command, people under fire are seldom inclined to argue over who should command, so long as the commander seems to know what he, or she, is doing. There were one or two among them who were admittedly just chauvinistic enough to later be amazed that they hadn't protested but, as the MP sergeant observed, "Jessie Thompson was neither chicken nor stupid. She wasn't just a brave woman, she was one hell of a soldier."

The Army command saw things slightly differently, however. First Lieutenant Jessica Thompson was something of an embarrassment to them. Women weren't supposed to fight in combat. But not everyone felt that way. One Army lieutenant colonel named Brown thought she ought to get a Distinguished Service Cross at a minimum. The people she had commanded during the long day and longer night were inclined to believe she should be the first woman to win the Medal of Honor. The generals who decided such things didn't agree. After much arguing among themselves, they finally gave Jessie Thompson a Silver Star and sent her home to Texas.

There was pressure from the Pentagon to forget the whole thing, and in the confusion that was Tet, there were enough male heros for the press and television to glorify that it was not too difficult to persuade a still cooperative media that Jessica G. Thompson should be quietly forgotten in the best interests of preserving the American military establishment, especially when official records listed the award as having been presented merely to "Thompson, J.G., 1st Lt., USAF."

But for all that, the chairborne commandos, safe in the Pentagon, could not change history. The important people, those who were there and survived, knew the truth; and the facts, no matter how disguised, nor how deeply buried, remained facts and were a matter of record.

Jessie Thompson was not sure what the nature of the security job advertised by the Texas-American Oil Company might be, but she was sure she had grown tired of having her bottom pinched by drunks.

Jessie pulled the battered and scarred case of her well-used portable typewriter out of the hall closet, hunted through a cardboard box of old papers until she found the documents she wanted, opened another Coke, and sat down at the kitchen table with the newspaper ad close at hand.

She ran her fingertips along her leg, feeling the scar. It wasn't so bad, she told herself. It was better than waiting tables and having drunks feel up your ass. She fed a sheet of paper into the machine and began to write.

HISTORICAL PERSPECTIVE:

On February 11, 1836, the morale of the
Texans at the Alamo took a giant leap upward. Davy
Crockett and a small band of men from Tennessee rode
in, pledging their loyalty to Texas. Suddenly, the men at
the Alamo believed that they were unbeatable. Both
Jim Bowie and Davy Crockett were with them. Santa
Anna was doomed.

The men wanted to throw a party for
Crockett, but Travis wouldn't let them. Rumors had
been flying for the last few days that the Mexicans
were close. Travis was afraid they would get caught in
the open during the party.

But, the Mexicans didn't arrive. Rumor was
that the Mexicans were still south of the Rio Grande.
Travis finally consented to a party. Santa Anna,
through his spies in San Antonio, learned of the party
and sent a large unit of cavalry ahead, hoping to catch
the Texans outside the fort. Unfortunately for them, an
early spring rain made the roads slippery and pushed a
few streams over their banks. Eight miles from San

Antonio, the Mexicans stalled.

The next morning, February 23, 1836, started ominously. Townspeople were leaving San Antonio in droves, carrying everything they could. For weeks people had been leaving, but this was something new. Travis pulled some of them aside, trying to find out what was happening, but they gave him lame excuses. He ordered a halt to the exodus, but that only made things worse. At 11:00 a.m., someone finally told the truth. A courier from Santa Anna had arrived during the night and told them to leave.

Travis went directly to the San Fernando Church. Its tower dominated the land around it. Carefully, Travis scanned the rolling hills and prairies but could see nothing. He posted a lookout and gave him orders to ring the bell if he spotted anything, or anyone. Travis then went back to his room.

Halicar, HISTORIAN
First Assistant to the Chief Archivist

FOUR

When Jessica G. Thompson entered the Texas-American Oil Company's corporate headquarters, she didn't know that the security manager had two offices. One was for applicants who would be carefully screened for hiring. The other one was for the applicants who would not be hired, based on either their appearance or their resumes. Thompson's appearance immediately disqualified her. She was a woman.

That didn't mean she wasn't attractive. In fact, Michael Travis, who had replaced the security manager, found her very exciting as he asked her to take a seat in the brown leather chair directly opposite his glass-topped, chrome-legged "tastefully modern" desk. The main reason for the glass top was that it allowed him to see the legs of all the female applicants.

Trying to maintain a conservative attitude, Thompson sat down, hoping that her closely tailored suit that had cost more than her budget could afford, would convince the recruiter that she was both professional and intelligent. Her skirt came to mid-knee but had a disco flair in the short split that revealed part of her thigh when she moved. The jacket accented her body without being obvious. She had brushed her hair until it shone and then cursed the wind and the rain as she ran to her car. She had set the light blue briefcase, another copy of her resume, her military records, and her medals, on the floor near her foot. She waited for Travis to speak.

He opened a pink folder muttering something about pink for the girls and blue for the boys.

While he inspected the papers, Thompson wondered if coming to the Texas-American Oil Company had been a good idea. She knew that corporate America was trying to change its image, but pink and blue folders seemed excessive.

"Very interesting resume, Jessica. May I call you that?"

"Surely." Why not, she added mentally.

Travis rocked in his high-backed executive chair, his elbows on its arms and his fingertips joined under his chin. "I see you're applying for one of our security jobs."

"Yes. As you can see, I have served in combat, leading a small unit in the Tet Offensive of 1968. I have included there, and brought with me, another copy of the citation I received after that action." She chose her words carefully, realizing that no one was going to accept her combat role at face value.

"I have read that interesting document. I confess that I was surprised. I hadn't known that women were involved in the Vietnam War."

"Normally they weren't. Naturally the Army and the Air Force had nurses in many of the combat zones. There were a few of us serving in other capacities in Saigon, Bien Hoa, and Da Nang. My own field was so specialized that they just didn't have anyone to send but me."

Travis nodded, peeking over his fingers and through the desktop at her legs, deciding that they were very good. "Then you spent all your time in rear areas?"

"Actually, there were no rear areas. Charlie moved with virtual impunity. During the day he might be a worker on the air base and at night lobbing mortar rounds at the aircraft."

"Yes, I suppose so."

"And, of course, as the citation explains, he was overrunning Tan Son Nhut when I received my award."

"I notice that it says, Thompson, J.G."

For an instant she was angry, but quickly squashed the feeling, explaining patiently, "That was so the Air Force could avoid the embarrassment of a woman leading its men in combat."

Travis smiled and nodded slowly. "What other experience have you had?"

"Naturally, the Air Force sent us all to basic training. I'm a specialist in photo imagery with a background in intelligence work. Civilian education was . . ."

"I have that in the record here." Travis waved a hand as if to make her speak faster. "I was wondering what other combat or security experience you have."

"I thought that would be enough. I have led men under fire in combat."

"That is not the only requirement. I admit that your experiences in Vietnam are unique, but we had a more experienced man, er, person, in mind."

Thompson picked up her briefcase and as she opened it, she said, "I have a complete familiarity with many types of small arms, from revolvers to light automatic weapons. I understand the maintenance necessary for them. I have . . ."

"Where did you get that experience?"

"Some of it through the Air Force, and my father taught

me some of it. Mostly I received training with the NRA in firearms safety and care."

Travis made a mark in the folder and said, "I see."

"I have the certificates issued by the NRA with me," she said as she pulled several papers out of her briefcase.

"I don't need to see those." Travis scanned the folder. "Have you had any kind of security work?"

"No."

"Ah," Travis made another mark. "I take it that you are single."

"Yes."

"And your political beliefs?"

She hesitated, remembering the ad. "I believe that we have the best form of government, even though it makes mistakes." She hoped that was noncommittal enough.

"Good. Good." Travis was quiet as he looked over the papers, neatly aligning them as he turned them over. For several minutes he didn't look up.

Thompson surveyed the room. The carpeting was thick and she could see all the foot-prints left by the visitors during the morning. Behind Travis was a book-lined wall, but she couldn't see any of the titles. She was sure that they had been bought "by the box" for display rather than picked up slowly by someone who read them.

"Well," said Travis as he closed the folder, "we'll let you know."

"But you don't think so."

Travis removed his glasses and set them on the desk. "I'll be frank with you, Jessica. I don't think that you're quite what we had in mind for this position."

"Why not? I meet all the requirements which, I might add, are stacked heavily against women."

"I'm afraid," said Travis, as he stared at the floor through the glass of his desk, "that we were hoping for people who had several months of combat experience."

"I was in Vietnam for eleven months and twenty days."

"But you weren't involved in combat all the time. I would venture to say that you spent most of your time in an air-conditioned office studying pictures." Travis waved an impatient hand. "We're looking for people who were combat soldiers and not haphazard heroes."

"Mr. Travis, I might remind you that certain Federal laws now on the books prohibit you from refusing employment on the basis of sex."

"I am aware of that." Travis smiled. "But, that is for persons who meet all the qualifications for the position."

"But I do. Your refusal is based on an arbitrary policy that, as I said, is heavily weighted against women. I'm sure that the Civil Rights Commission would be interested."

"Jessica, I know that you're disappointed and are speaking in anger. You wouldn't want a job that you forced yourself into with threats of federal action. Think of the animosity that you would create. You'd then have to fight your way up the ladder, climbing over all those people who were sure that you were being promoted because you had caused trouble before. You wouldn't have a friend."

Thompson felt her anger build. She watched Travis put her folder into his out basket. She wanted to reach out for it and take it to someone other than the smug Personnel Manager because she knew she could do the job.

Travis stood. "I'll tell you what I'll do. I have a list of your talents. I'll keep my eyes open and see if we can find something more suited to you."

Thompson didn't move. She just stared at Travis, and when the door behind her opened, she didn't turn around to see who it was. The man stepped to the desk and asked, "Another applicant, Mike?"

"She was just leaving."

Thompson turned slightly. "I was not. I was explaining

to MISTER Travis, here, that we're no longer living in the 1950's and women are taking, and handling, jobs that were once reserved for men."

The man nodded and held out his hand. "I'm Robert Brown." He looked over his shoulder. "Let me see her file."

As he opened it, he stepped back, reading carefully. After a couple of minutes, he closed it and tossed it on the desk. "Hire her."

Travis exploded. "What? You can't just come in here and demand that . . ."

Brown spoke quietly but there was a hard edge to his voice. "Yes I can. My contract specifies it. Now hire her." He turned to Thompson. "We have your address and we'll be in touch within the week to fill out forms and let you know more about the job. You can be ready Monday?"

"Of course." Thompson stood and picked up her case and tried to shake hands with Brown while thanking him for the opportunity. He escorted her to the door and closed it when she left.

Travis said, "Now what the hell do you mean coming in here like that?"

Brown moved to the chair and sat. "I could ask you what the hell do you mean screening out applicants without my knowing about it."

Sure of his ground, Travis said, "We always do that. We know what qualifications are needed and screen those who don't meet them. Thompson didn't meet them."

"Okay. We can knock that crap off right now. I will see all the applicants for the special security position. I said that I would pick the team and I mean that. If I hadn't asked your secretary what you were doing, you would have let one fine prospect get away. Not to mention probably getting us involved in a suit with the Government, which is the last thing we need. I'm sure Lewis wouldn't like that."

Before he spoke, Travis moved to his chair. He picked up Thompson's folder and then slammed it to his desk. "All right, Brown, now I'll tell you something. I don't like you coming in here and overriding my decisions. Next time, you'll ask my secretary to buzz me, and I'll ask you in when business has been completed."

Brown took a deep breath. "Just leave the hiring of my people to me. Period." He stood and went to the door. "And that's the way it will be."

FIVE

Brown tossed his pencil on the papers in front of him, watched it bounce to the floor, and then shut the folder. He realized that the walls were beginning to close in on him. If he got up from the wobbly chair in front of the combination desk-dresser-luggage rack of his hotel room, the only place to sit would be the bed, and it somehow seemed obscene to be sitting on the bed at seven. In fact, the whole thing was beginning to seem obscene.

He knew that he had to get some air. It didn't matter where he went, as long as it was outside the hotel. With the map that came in the rented Ford to guide him, Brown headed for the suburbs. He drove up and down the main streets looking for something interesting and when he saw the All American Bar with its "Totally Girl Revue" he recognized the name. It had been in one of the personnel folders that he had been studying.

The inside was what he had expected. Fairly dark with a raised, lighted stage near the center of the large room. A long bar, with a giant mirror behind it, dominated one end of the place. A tall blonde who was wearing nothing but a pair of sandals and miniature bikini bottom was bouncing to the music while a dozen old men cheered wildly and tried to get her to dance toward them so that they could slip dollar bills into her pants.

Brown found a table in a corner and watched the waitresses in abbreviated costumes wander among the men who ignored them so that they could concentrate on the girl on stage. When a waitress swung close to him, he ordered a dark beer and idly watched the dancer.

Out of the corner of his eye he thought he saw a familiar face and looked in time to see Jessica Thompson put three beers on the table next to him. She smiled as she picked up the money and as she turned, one of the customers reached over and pinched her so hard that she jumped. Instead of saying anything, she moved away quickly.

At the bar she looked back at the men, and Brown stood to wave. She caught the signal and headed for his table, detouring around the three drunks.

At first Thompson didn't know who he was, but when recognition dawned she smiled awkwardly and asked if there was anything that he needed.

"I've ordered." He pointed at the chair opposite him. "Why don't you sit for a minute?"

"Can't. Management won't let the waitresses sit with the customers. The show girls can. It's sort of a status symbol." She put her wet tray on the table and leaned on the back of the chair.

"Sit anyway. All they can do is fire you, and I happen to know that you have a better job lined up."

"If it lasts, which I doubt. I want to keep the management happy so that I can get this job back if I need it."

Brown shrugged and sat down. "Somehow I can't think

of this as a job that anyone would want to preserve."

Anger flared in her eyes. "Easy for you to say. You've got a job and it's not because of your ability. Part of it is because you're a man. I've tried for other jobs, but because I'm female, they think that I should sit out front and type and file. Hell, I type with two fingers. Never had a need to learn."

For a moment Brown was at a loss for words. Finally he said, "Aren't you being a little too defensive? I'm sure that you could find better work if you weren't so busy feeling sorry for yourself."

Thompson pulled out a chair and sat. She glared across the table and said in a low voice that trembled with her anger, "It's so easy for you to sit there and judge, isn't it? You haven't had to scramble to be better. Any job I take, or have had, I had to be better than the men. Everyone expected me to fail and when I didn't, they were surprised, and then attributed it to luck, or the help of the males near me.

"You saw Travis try to keep me out of the security job, and you can't tell me it was anything but my sex. That whole program is purposely loaded against women, and I know why they did it."

Brown sipped the cold beer and set the glass down carefully. His eyes were on it and not Thompson. "I'm afraid you're wrong about the job."

"Oh, I am? I suppose you know all about it."

"Of course. I wrote the ad." He held up a hand to stop her protest. "No, I didn't think about discrimination when I wrote it. The only thought I had in mind was that I wanted combat veterans. The job, as it was explained to me, seemed to demand that requirement. I didn't think it would put any one group at a disadvantage. In fact, I've hired four other women since you."

"And how many men?"

"Eighteen. But we naturally get fewer women responding."

Thompson pulled the wet rag from her tray and unconsciously wiped at the table. "But you don't expect the women to succeed. They're hired to fill the government requirements."

Brown felt tired. He knew the argument wasn't going to go anywhere, but he persisted. "I have no such expectations. I don't expect everyone to complete the training. And yes, I would have reservations about placing women in some of the assignments that I anticipate, but that reservation is based on cultural bias and not on a conception of ability."

"I guess I can't expect a man to understand how it is."

"I suppose not. But I sometimes wonder if you, meaning all the minorities, don't read discrimination into the most innocent of acts."

Thompson tossed the rag at the tray, aware for the first time that she was sitting. "You have never had a job where promotion was based on sleeping with the boss. Or having all the men in the office assume that you want to play touchy-feely with them because they are so magnificent. When I was in the Air Force, I don't know how many times the other officers would bring me papers to type assuming I could type because I was a woman. Or they would ask me to sew a button on their uniforms. You have no idea . . ."

"I guess I don't. Look, Jessica, I'm sorry about all that. All I can say is that I won't give you any papers to type. I've tried to treat all the people under my command as equals, assuming nothing about them."

She looked at him carefully, aware of the steel blue eyes and the smattering of grey hair. "I suppose I can't ask for more than that."

One of the drunks staggered up to the table, putting his hand on her shoulder, but as he weaved to maintain his balance, he managed to slip it to her breast. Brown started to stand and then dropped back into his chair as he realized that this was the type of automatic defense of her that she had been talking about. If she needed his help, he was sure that she would ask for it, but he would not offer it until it was needed. If it was needed.

Thompson turned, pulling back slightly. The drunk's hand moved to the back of the chair. "We'd like some service."

Thompson's smile was painted on. "Of course. Be right with you."

"And bring yourself a drink and sit with us."

"I'm not allowed to sit with the customers."

"Is that all the customers, or only us?" The drunk looked toward Brown.

"She's my cousin."

The drunk hitchhiked a thumb over his shoulder. "Well, cousin Tom over there would like a drink with the l'il lady. And I would like a l'il kiss. We're kissin' cousins." He smiled at his own wit.

Thompson ducked under the man's puckered lips and stood up, grabbing at her tray and towel. "I'll be with you in just a minute."

He reached for her and moved toward her. Thompson sidestepped him easily and as he went by, she pushed him. He stumbled, bumped a table, and fell into a woman's lap, ripping her dress. She screamed and hit at him as her escort shot around the table to pluck the man up and toss him back the way he came.

The other two men stood and started moving toward Thompson, but the bouncer intercepted them. They saw that there was nothing they could do except help their friend to his feet. The bouncer suggested that the management would like to buy the next round, if they would quietly wait at their table.

The men grumbled but went away. Thompson leaned close to Brown and mumbled something that was lost in the sound from the jukebox which had been turned up to mask the noise of the altercation. The manager came from behind the bar. He stopped Thompson, talked to her quietly and took her tray. She went back to the table and looked at Brown.

"I'm fired."

"It's probably for the best."

"It wasn't a bad job. It paid well and the tips were very good. It gave me my days off and didn't demand a lot."

"I'll buy you a drink, then. You go on our payroll Monday."

She looked at him closely, wondering if it was a come-on, but there was nothing in his face to give her a clue. She said, "Not here. And not dressed like this."

"Do you have any other clothes here?"

"No. I'll have to go home to change. Do you have a car?"

Brown nodded.

"You can follow me. I'll change and then we'll get a drink."

Four hours later Brown unlocked the door to his room. He walked in and tossed the key onto the bed, wondering about Thompson. Her apartment had been small but neat. They had been there only ten minutes. She had changed rapidly and her nervousness seemed to evaporate when they left. Thompson's anger over being fired had slowly dissipated after three Bloody Marys. As they talked, it became obvious that she was glad to have been fired. The job really hadn't been as good as she claimed.

They had decided to have dinner and a final drink.

Brown had driven her home and at the door it had somehow seemed natural to kiss her goodnight. He had sensed
her surprise when he didn't accept her offer of a nightcap.
He had surprised himself, as well, and it wasn't until he
was sitting in his car that he realized that he had violated
one of his rules. Of course, Thompson wasn't under his
command yet, but it was still a good policy. One shouldn't
date the women one commanded. But, it hadn't been a
date. Teenagers dated.

Brown fell back on the bed, his hands under his head as
he stared at the ceiling. Why, he wondered, was he working so hard at rationalizing the evening with Thompson? It
had been a coincidence and nothing more. It had been nice
even if it was coincidence.

HISTORICAL PERSPECTIVE:

For hours the guard that Travis had left in the church tower saw nothing. However, at 2:00 in the afternoon, he rang the bell. Travis and a number of other Texas officers scrambled into the tower but could see nothing. The sentry claimed that he had seen mounted men in the distance. Most of the officers refused to believe him.

Dr. John Sutherland and John W. Smith wanted to ride out to check the story. They didn't think they would find anything, but it was better than sitting in San Antonio with nothing to do. Travis arranged a simple code with them. if they rode back at anything other than a walk, it meant that the Mexicans were close.

Less than half a mile out of town, they spotted a Mexican cavalry unit which Sutherland estimated to be made up of least 1500 men. Records show that there were no more than 400 men in this advance unit, but actual numbers were not as important as the fact that the Mexican army was near. Sutherland and Smith turned to race back to the Alamo, but Sutherland's horse slipped in the mud, throwing him. Sutherland twisted his knee, but was able to ride. They continued to San Antonio.

The sentry saw them coming and relayed the signal to the streets. All over San Antonio, the Texans began leaving houses, cantinas, stores, and churches, running up the streets, crossing the small footbridge, and entering the Alamo. Travis went to the small room on the west wall that was his headquarters and scribbled a brief note to Fannin in Goliad, hoping that he could pry part of the Texas army out of there in time for them to help. A courier named Johnson took the message and rode out.

As Johnson left, Davy Crockett and John Sutherland came in. Travis realized that the doctor wasn't going to be much help during the siege because of his injured knee, and sent him to Gonzales in an attempt to rally help there.

Travis then turned to Crockett and gave him the toughest assignment. Travis told Crockett to take his twelve men to the southeastern part of the fort, near the chapel, and defend the earth and wood barricade that had been built there. It was the weakest point in the defenses.

Halicar, HISTORIAN
First Assistant to the Chief Archivist

SIX

For three hours Sage Williamson had followed Tucker around the lab, trying to learn everything he could about the operation of the Tucker Transfer. Fortunately, Tucker didn't seem to be one of those secretive scientists who jealously guarded their discoveries. Tucker was only too happy to explain, at length, how everything worked.

Williamson jumped into a pause in Tucker's explanation of the inverse induction coils and said, "Fascinating. Is there a chance that I could have another practical demonstration?"

"Not this afternoon."

"Why not?"

"Temperature. Must be ninety-five out there."

"Does that adversely affect the machine?"

Tucker stopped talking and looked at Williamson. "Haven't you been listening? Not directly. However, air conditioning will be at its peak use in about twelve minutes, and the power needed to run that and the equipment

53

puts too much strain on the entire electrical grid. We could knock out the power."

"You mean here in the lab?"

"I mean all over. You remember the May blackout that covered Texas, Louisiana, Mississippi, and Oklahoma?"

"You did that?"

"Not all by myself, but the strain we put onto the grid caused the local power company to draw heavily from surrounding areas until . . . I guess you don't want to hear all that. Anyway, if we try anything now, before the peak load has decreased, we'll black out the area again. After midnight is the best time."

Williamson laughed. "This is incredible. You mean to say that you now delay your experiments until after midnight because of air conditioning?"

"Yes. Basically."

"Could we run through the sequence once anyway?"

"Sure."

After they ran through it, Williamson said casually, "I think Travis and Lewis are going to want you in Dallas to make a report."

"But they know everything we've done here."

"Your experiments haven't progressed?"

Tucker walked to the green chair and sat down. He found a package of cigars, took one out, lighted it carefully, and tossed the match over his shoulder. It went into the ashtray as if it had eyes. "If you mean, have we sent a man back, the answer is no. We haven't even reached the stage of sending animals. There are some things that we still have to check before we use animals."

"You don't have to go to Dallas for six or seven weeks. It would be nice to have some dramatic results for Mr. Lewis."

"We have a timetable and I can see no need to rush anything."

Williamson smiled. "Of course not. I was only suggesting that the first experiments with animals would be a nice climax. Build your presentation to a powerful ending. I'm available to assist in some of it."

Tucker smoked quietly, his eyes closed. "Actually, that shouldn't be too difficult. We have nearly completed all the work that would lead to the first transfer of an animal."

"That's fine. Mr. Lewis would like you to brief him and a few members of the board on August 2. You can give your staff the day off. Let them have a long weekend. Send them to Padre Island or something."

Tucker leaned forward over the tray just as the ash fell from his cigar. He frowned at his watch. He had read somewhere that a good cigar could go fifteen minutes before it needed an ashtray. This one had barely made ten. "I don't see any problems. Nor can I see a need to speed up the research to please the people in Dallas."

Williamson agreed. He also made a mental note that he would have to stay here so that he could guide the research slightly. Not all the time. Only enough so that they would be ready on August 2.

SEVEN

Fifty-seven prospective security guards assembled in the wooden bleachers overlooking a large, rocky valley on 890 acres of Texas-American owned land southwest of Dallas. There was a partial roof over the bleachers that threw a little shade on the top two rows. Nearly everyone sat in the late morning sun waiting for a corporate official to tell them what to do.

Brown stood next to Travis in the guard shack fifty yards away, sipping coffee and watching the stands. He was trying to evaluate the people who had applied for, and who had been hired temporarily as, security guards.

He turned at the sound behind him and saw the guard sitting at the console flip through a sequence that gave him a televised view of nearly all the 890 acres. When he finished, the guard said, "They're about a hundred yards out."

"All right, Travis, keep your eyes open now and tell me your reactions." Brown spoke to the guard. "You'll get this all on video tape?"

"Yes sir. No problem."

"Focus on the stands. It's the first minute or so that I'll be interested in."

Both Travis and Brown crowded to the small window so that they could see the bleachers. The guard started the tape and said, "About thirty yards."

Outside, the men and women sat facing away from the tiny force that was stalking them, totally unaware of the surprise. They had been told that training would start at 10:00 and that they should be in place by then. They had all checked into the Texas-American Security Training site the night before. The brochures had claimed they would spend six weeks learning the ins and outs of security work and receive an orientation to the country where they would probably be stationed. Now they were grumbling because it was after 10:00 and no one had showed up to start anything.

Jim McGee looked at the woman sitting next to him and said, "This is really crap. Make us come in a day early so that we won't be late, and then they don't bother showing."

"Yeah, everyone's time is more important than ours."

The crash of an artillery simulator caught them all by surprise. McGee didn't look around. He pitched out of the bleachers, landing on his stomach in the tall grass where he could see what was happening. Not far away were several huge trees that receded into good cover in small woods. He began working his way to them.

Jessie Thompson, who had been sitting in the third row, leaped over the first two and tried to roll under the bleachers. She saw movement behind them, where the ground level dropped away, and began crawling rapidly in the opposite direction.

Shooting broke out around them as the men in the attack force started firing blanks. They were up and running now, trying to add to the confusion of the people in the stands.

In the guard hut, Brown pointed to a man standing on the bleachers looking around wildly. "Fire him."

Travis nodded and wrote down a name.

A man and woman had climbed the bleachers and were watching the show, pointing and laughing. Brown indicated them. "And both of them."

"I don't know the man, yet, but I'll get his name," said Travis as he wrote.

To the left, Brown saw two men crawling through the grass, heading toward one of the attackers. He didn't say anything to Travis. He just mentally noted it and hoped that no one would be seriously hurt because he thought he knew what was going to happen.

The two men separated and circled, popping out of the grass at the same time. Their target apparently didn't see them at first as he fired in the air. One of the men jumped for the attacker's arm, trying to wrestle the rifle from him, while the other leaped on him to keep him too busy to fight for the gun. The attacker surrendered immediately.

By now everyone in the stands had reacted to the attack. Forty-two of the potential special security guards had passed the test. Travis had marked down eleven names. Those were the people he had recognized. He would compare the video tape with pictures to identify the other four. All fifteen would be terminated by 3:00 that afternoon and would be offered regular security jobs in Texas-American so they wouldn't be inclined to complain.

The trainees returned to the bleachers. Many of them were dirty and a few had torn clothes. Brown smiled at that. It meant that some of the influences of civilization were ignored by the people who wanted to be on his team. They wouldn't worry about clean clothes, or going out in the rain, or not bathing for a week at a time. All were good signs.

When they had settled, Brown said, "First, let me welcome you to this training camp. I'm sorry that your initial exercise was so surprising, but we needed to evaluate your reaction time, and it seemed to us that you would be most vulnerable to such an exercise just before your training program started. I'm happy to say that most of you passed with flying colors."

For twenty minutes Brown went through the opening speech that had been prepared for him by the Texas-American Graphic Services Department. There were a number of flip charts that could be used to add emphasis where he wanted it. Travis had insisted on them. Brown ignored them.

By 11:00, he had finished. He asked for questions and answered them until Travis walked up and handed him two sheets of paper. Brown read them to himself before he said, "Those people whose names I'm about to read should meet with Mr. Travis during lunch."

When he finished the first list, he scanned the shorter, second list. It contained the names of the people who had reacted with above average intelligence during the raid. It included McGee, because he had reached the woods; Thompson, because she had gotten away by crawling out of the battle area; and the two men, Lemuel Crawford and James Hannum, who had jumped the attacker. After he read the names, he said, "I would like to see each of you after you finish your lunch. Are there any quick questions?"

At 2:00, they reassembled, minus the fifteen who had failed the test. The remainder had been divided into four squads, with the four people who had done the best on the test taking over as temporary squad leaders.

The afternoon was passed with preliminaries. Brown wanted each of the people to talk about backgrounds, impressions, and desires for the future. It was a time-consuming process but at the end of it, he had added two more names to the termination list.

That night they were assigned to barracks, with Thompson in charge of the other five women. It made the arrangements difficult because the camp hadn't been laid out with women in mind, but it was worked out. The next morning, training began for real.

They didn't have to start from scratch. Every one of them had combat experience or military type training and were familiar with many of the things that Brown thought necessary for his force. They started beyond basic training. They started beyond the basic moves of karate, beyond target practice, and beyond precision drill. They went straight to the methods of killing a sentry without noise. Straight to infiltrating enemy lines, and straight to long-range sniping. And, even though each of those skills was not something expected of the normal security guard, no one asked why they were learning them. After all, the Texas-American Oil Company was paying well, and the skills could come in handy if they were posted to guard oil fields in some of the unstable areas of the world.

And so, the training progressed. They went through combat firing courses that demanded quick reactions and quick thought. Two people were eliminated when they couldn't complete the course fast enough. They went through an obstacle course that demanded agility and physical strength. One man was eliminated. They went through a night firing course, and another man was eliminated when it was discovered that he was night-blind.

After five weeks, they were down to twenty-six men and two women. Brown, with the help of Travis, organized a small graduation ceremony, held near the bleachers where they had had the first test. For a few days, Brown had thought that he should try one more test, another attack, but he decided that the graduates would be expecting it. If they weren't, then the whole program had been a waste.

After each was given a certificate on which Travis had insisted, designed by a Texas-American commercial artist, Brown made a short speech. He stood behind a wooden lectern that had been supplied for the graduation and stared into the afternoon sun, trying to read from notes that were continually blown about by a strong, warm breeze. Finally he gave up, folded the notes into the pocket of his fatigues, and said, "During the next week, we will be examining our assignments before we are sent overseas. It will be somewhat different than you expect. But after living with all of you for the last five weeks, I don't think it is something that you will find distasteful. Initial briefings will begin at zero eight hundred."

Brown wiped sweat from his forehead. "I know that you're all as hot and miserable as I am, so just let me say, our relationship changed this afternoon. I no longer think of you as trainees. You are now colleagues. I'm not going to tell you that you have work to do here tonight. In fact, the old military type training you have experienced is at an end. You are free to do as you please until 8:00 Monday. I'll expect each of you to be here, on time and sober."

As he turned to walk away, Brown looked back over his shoulder. "That's it. Take off."

There was a shout as everyone faded from sight. They didn't want to be caught by one of Brown's training exercises, even though he said they were over. And, having learned from the military that you never hang around when you are told to leave because someone might find something for you to do, they vanished.

HISTORICAL PERSPECTIVE:

A little after 3:00, Sutherland rode out of town and fell in with Smith again. Smith wanted to go to Gonzales to recruit help, so the men rode together. On a rise just east of town, they stopped to look back and saw Mexican soldiers pouring into the Military Plaza. Santa Anna's troops had arrived.

The joint command of Travis and Bowie was still in effect when the first units of Santa Anna's army arrived, but records indicate that Bowie sent word that he wanted to talk. He hadn't notified Travis. To show his irritation, Travis did the same. In the first few hours of the siege, the problem of command still needed to be solved.

It made no difference who sent representatives to talk to the Mexicans. The message was basically the same. Santa Anna wanted unconditional surrender, and neither Travis nor Bowie planned on surrender under any terms. The messengers, after a long talk, returned to the Alamo.

Moments later, a blast from the Alamo's 18-pounder told the Mexicans that surrender was unacceptable. The siege was officially on.

During the rest of the afternoon, Mexican soldiers rode and marched into San Antonio. A loose ring was thrown around the fort, but the units were so widely scattered that it did little to isolate the Alamo. In fact, Santa Anna never succeeded in completely isolating the fort. Couriers, most notably James Butler Bonham, rode in and out of the fort to the very end.

The last message of the day seemed to be the flag that one of the advance units raised over the church where only hours earlier the Texans had stationed their sentries. Now flapping in the light afternoon breeze was a blood-red banner of Spanish origin. It meant that no quarter would be given to the defenders of the Alamo. When the fort was taken, all the defenders would die.

Sutherland and Smith heard Travis' response to the flag. One shot from the 18-pounder. They may even have seen the flag. Both turned and galloped for Gonzales, sure that they could raise a large force to relieve the Alamo.

As the sun dropped toward the horizon, Santa Anna finally rode into town with part of his army. He entered the Yturri house, a strong one-story building that had been used by the Texans as an outpost. Without a word to anyone, he began organizing the siege.

Halicar, HISTORIAN
First Assistant to the Chief Archivist

EIGHT

Travis sat in the corporate board room, relishing the coolness that was being blown at him from the air conditioner. Texas-American had a solar generating plant, a windmill, and its own gasoline generator, so they didn't have to rely on the local power company. Because of all that, they had ignored most of the Federal Government's demands that everyone cut back their air conditioning.

Without a word, H. Perot Lewis entered through the door that connected with his office and took the chair at the head of the conference table. He reached for the water pitcher that was set near his end of the table and poured a glass. After he drained it, he said, "What now, Mike?"

Travis opened the manila folder that was in front of him. He leaned both elbows on the table and said, "Our last figures, based on what Sage Williamson learned in Gonzales, show that we might black out a great portion of the Southwest if we try a transfer of the magnitude we need."

65

"Uh-huh. Has anyone thought of splitting the loads?"

"Well, yes. But, we don't want to try to send the mercenaries in small groups. We might surprise the first bunch, but the odds are that we couldn't persuade the rest to go. Besides, the reduction in the size of the group doesn't lower the power requirements by all that much."

Lewis leaned back, closed his eyes, and pinched the bridge of his nose as he wondered why they made him come up with all the solutions. Quietly, he said, "Anyone thought about providing the power ourselves?"

"We looked into that, but the time it would take to build the facilities prohibits it. Unless you want to push the timetable back by nine to fourteen months."

"No way." Privately, he thought, not enough time, but to Travis he said, "We can't afford to let this sit that long. There would surely be a leak."

"There is one other problem."

"What's that?"

"We can assume that we're going to black out, at the very least, east Texas. Given the time of the year, and the length of time the power will be off, which depends on how big an area loses power, we project fifteen to sixty-two deaths."

"What in the hell are you talking about?"

Travis pushed a graph across the highly polished surface of the table. "We assume that the power outage will last about three hours. In that case, air conditioning will be off; power to homes, where electrical medical equipment is used, will be off. So on and so forth. While most homes that have need of medical equipment have backup systems, three hours is a long time. Some people are going to die. And, August is the worst time to lose air conditioning. Some elderly and some of the very young are going to die."

"You're sure?"

"I can show you the figures. I can show you what happened in 1979 during a massive blackout in the Houston area. It was down-played by the press, but there were a few deaths."

"Okay. What's our liability?"

Travis leafed through his papers. "That's an interesting question. Naturally, we don't want anything in writing, so these notes will be shredded.

"But, to get back. I don't see any way that this can be traced to us. The power company's records will show the lab's use at a certain level. If it suddenly goes up, as it will when we begin the Transfer, there may be an overload that causes the blackout, but it won't be traced to us."

Lewis nodded. "Let me get this straight. You say that we'll knock out the power and that there will undoubtedly be deaths, but you say they won't be traced to us?"

"That's right."

Lewis stood. "Then go. As long as we won't catch any flack."

"We won't."

"How soon will we send them?"

"Williamson says that he knows enough now to run the Transfer. If something goes wrong, we may lose the people, but Williamson can handle almost everything. Training for the mercenaries is about finished. Still have to go through the horsemanship, and some of the weapons are still being bought, but everything is on schedule. We go on schedule."

"Keep me briefed."

HISTORICAL PERSPECTIVE:

The joint-command problem solved itself
early on February 24. Bowie, meeting with Travis in
the Alamo headquarters, suddenly collapsed. He had
been sick all winter and the effects had finally caught
up with him. He called several of his friends, told Travis
to take overall command, and then asked to be carried
to his room. He told his sister-in-law, who had followed
him into San Antonio, not to worry. Colonel Travis and
Colonel Crockett would take care of her.

Throughout the night the men of the Alamo
could hear the Mexicans moving outside the walls. In
the distance men were talking, some joking, arms were
stacked and supplies arranged. There were sounds of
construction, hammering and digging. When it was
light, they could see that the Mexicans had built an
earthwork on the river bank only 400 yards from the
fort, out of rifle range, but not cannon range.

Throughout the cloudy day, the Mexicans
bombarded the fort. The Texans, worried about the

amount of powder they had, returned fire only occasionally. Most of the day they crouched behind the walls, in irrigation ditches, or in the chapel, waiting. They weren't sure what they were waiting for, but it was about the only thing they could do. Travis tried to keep up their spirits, telling them that Fannin would arrive soon. It may have been bravado because the tone of his messages suggested that he knew help would never arrive in time.

As night fell, the cannonade ceased. Travis took time to scribble another message and gave it to Albert Martin. Martin rode out and wasn't even chased by the Mexican cavalry. He was too far away when they finally saw him.

Halicar, HISTORIAN
First Assistant to the Chief Archivist

NINE

Three days later, Brown sat on the top of a rough wooden corral fence, watching the members of his team chase horses around in an attempt to saddle them. This was the one item of training that both Travis and Lewis had insisted upon although Brown couldn't figure out what was important about learning to ride. In one of the staff meetings, Travis had fought for the point and they had compromised. Brown would not make it part of his training, but if the corporation wanted it included, they could hire someone to teach it to the mercenaries, after Brown had completed his course.

Brown, after his experiences in Rhodesia, knew how to ride. A close friend, Denny Wilson, had taken pains to make sure that Brown understood all the finer points of horsemanship. Most of the pain, however, had been Brown's. He had been thrown at least a hundred times before he got good at it.

These horses, however, were tame compared to the ones

that Brown had learned on. Most of the mercenaries were able to walk up carefully, holding a hand out as if it held sugar, and slip on the bridle. They then could throw the saddle on the horse's back and tighten the cinch. They could even climb up on the wrong side. The horses ignored them.

The riding instructor stood in the center of the corral, slowly spinning so that he could yell at everyone in turn. He told them to be careful with the bridles, to loosen the cinches, to tighten the cinches, and to mount from the left side. He told them not to give the horses sugar because they would get worms, but that carrots might be nice.

Brown searched for Thompson and saw her on the other side of the corral, sitting on her horse and watching the others struggle. She was smiling at some of the antics. She pulled one foot out of the stirrup and hooked her leg over the saddle horn so that she could lean her forearm on her leg. With her other hand she pushed her hat back on her head and wiped the sweat away.

Brown stared at her for a moment wondering about her. During the training he had remained slightly aloof, not because he felt he was better than her, but because she was in training. And, because she was one of the squad leaders, and as it turned out, one of the best recruits, he found that he couldn't stay away from her. They had to work closely. Brown found that he leaned on her, because what she didn't know, she learned quickly, and then could teach it to others who weren't quite so fast. Thompson turned out to be one of the most valuable of the mercenaries. And one of the smartest.

He sat there, the sweat rolling down his face and sides, remembering an evening they spent together. He had told himself several times, it was nothing. But, during the three days that the mercenaries had been out of Texas-American control, Brown had missed her. Not missed her, really, but wished that she was around.

He had wanted her to be around so that she would be, around. It was something that he hadn't experienced in a very long time, and he was mildly irritated at himself for what he thought of as a weakness.

There was no denying that Thompson was attractive. Brown had never seen eyes so blue. More importantly, she seemed to share many of his interests. If she didn't, she would never have contacted Texas-American for the job interview. She took to the training. She excelled at it. She was intelligent. And, Brown discovered, he had just gone over that, for the second time.

The instructor, still standing ankle-deep in some of the best fertilized soil in Texas, was trying to form the mercenaries into a long file so that they could ride around in a big circle to get the feel of the horses under them. He continued to shout instructions, corrections and obscenities.

As Thompson rode by, Brown waved her over. He leaned an elbow on the fence-post next to him. "You've ridden before?"

"My father again. Taught me to use a rifle, clean and dress game, play chess and baseball. And, he said that any girl from Texas had to know how to ride. Sort of an unwritten rule."

"Well, like everything else, you do it quite well."

"Why, thank you Colonel."

He smiled at that. There had been a hint of sarcasm in her voice but also a trace of good humor. He didn't let it bother him. To change the subject, he said, "I guess we surprised you. Didn't fire you and make you go back to waiting tables."

"Mildly. Just mildly. After talking to you that night, I knew I could count on a fair shake. I'm a little surprised that Texas-American let you push them into it."

"No problem there. I insisted on complete control over my people before I took the job." He stopped talking, realizing that he didn't really have anything to say. For an instant he felt like a high school boy talking to the head cheerleader.

Thompson slipped off the horse and sat next to him on the fence. "If you don't mind, I think I'll sit out for a minute."

"No problem. Unless you feel the need to practice riding."

"Colonel," she said hesitantly. "Colonel, I have a question to ask. It's been bothering me for quite a while."

Brown turned to look at her closely. "Ask away."

"In Vietnam, after Tet, when the Air Force and the government were arguing over my medal, I heard rumors that there was an Army officer who thought that I should be put in for the Medal of Honor, and then practically put his career on the line trying to get me the DSC when the Pentagon East brass wouldn't go for the Congressional."

"Yes."

"Was that you?"

"I believe that it was."

"Oh." She didn't know what to say next. Finally she asked, "Is that why you hired me? Why you said that the waitress job was beneath my dignity?"

"Partially. That was one hell of a thing you pulled off at Tan Son Nhut. If you had been a man I'm sure that you would have gone in for the Medal of Honor. Hell, everyone was looking for heroes. Johnson and his crowd wanted some badly, but it wouldn't have looked right for a woman, girl really, to have led those big brave men in combat. It was a hell of a deal and you got the short end of it."

She smiled. "You've just explained quite a bit to me."

"Jessie, I'm going to violate one of my cardinal rules.

Normally, I try not to socialize with the people under my command, other than official functions and the like. I've often felt that I, by my presence, can kill a good party. No one wants to get loose with the boss there. That sort of thing. But, I'm going to take a chance that you're mature enough . . . Oh, hell, I'm botching this. Would you like to have dinner tonight?"

She hesitated and then said, "All right."

Brown started to speak, stopped and said, "I was going to make another dumb speech, but you don't need it. I'll call for you at seven."

Thompson climbed back on her horse. "I'll be ready. But I may smell like a stable."

Late in the afternoon, Brown walked over to the riding instructor. "Guess that's about it for today."

"Still have a good hour of work to do."

Brown shook his head. "Not today. I want to talk to my people. You wait in the barn, and I'll have them bring in their horses when we're finished."

When the man was gone, Brown signaled the mercenaries to halt and had them dismount. They stood next to their horses, holding the reins and squinting into the sun.

Brown surveyed them for a moment as he rubbed the sweat from the back of his neck. "There is an aspect of this job that I think we should discuss before we continue much further. I'm going to give you some details of the job that the company would probably prefer that I didn't. I'm doing it because I think I know each of you well enough to know that you'll do nothing to harm us, if any one of you decides that he or she wants out.

"There is no easy way to say this, other than just come out with it. I don't want any of it to go beyond here, however.

"As most of you have probably figured out by now, we

are not going to be security guards. Texas-American, for reasons of its own, wants us to prop up a force of rebel soldiers holding a small fort in a tiny African country."

McGee said, "Surprise. Surprise."

Brown ignored that. "We will form a cadre, help in the defense, and train the natives. The job will last between three and four weeks. We will all be well paid for our help, and Texas-American has promised to find good jobs for those of you who want to stay on with the company afterward.

"I have been promised that rescue helicopters and a large ship will be standing by, in case things in the country deteriorate to a point where we can't reverse it. I've worked out the details with the higher management."

"Is this a good idea, Colonel?" asked Jim Hannum.

"I've looked at the situation, and I believe that it is. It's really more than an oil company trying to engineer the world situation for its own benefit. I'll grant you that Texas-American will profit, but so will the people. I think that in the long run, it's a good idea."

Brown scanned the people. "Right now, I don't want to go into more detail, for security reasons. We'll have a full-scale briefing before we arrive on target. I'm telling you this now, in case some of you want to bail out. This is the time to quit, because once we leave the States, it will be too late.

"If, for any reasons, you want out, come and see me, privately. We'll work something out. Now, let's break early. Get your horses into the barn and we'll start again tomorrow, at the regular time."

Of course, Brown didn't know it at that time, but none of his people would ask to be let out. They all felt the same way Brown did, after the operational plan was fully explained to them. The change in Equatorial Guinea was better for its citizens then letting things go, and the mission appealed to their spirit of adventure. As McGee put it when Brown asked him later if he was sure everyone wanted to go, "Nothing for any of us here. Why the hell not?"

Now that the official training was over, everyone had been housed in a Ramada Inn about ten miles from the entrance to the training site. Across the street was a restaurant, built to cater to Texas-American brass who came frequently to inspect various training programs. Not that they were needed. But it was a good excuse to get away from home for a few days, and a lot of executives took advantage of it.

Brown and Thompson decided to eat at the hotel restaurant since it was the best in the tiny Texas town. Brown didn't care for the Muzak piped into the dining room, but then, nearly every building owner in the United States had been convinced by one hell of a salesman that it was a good idea.

After a long, leisurely dinner, they walked downtown and back out to the motel. It hadn't taken more than thirty minutes and they had walked slowly. At the door, Thompson, while fumbling for her key, asked Brown in, and this time, he said, "Yes."

There was a moment of uneasiness after Brown brought a container of ice back from the machine. Thompson was sitting in the only chair, waiting with the drinks made, lacking only the ice. Brown, who preferred to pour his liquor over the ice, didn't say anything. Instead, he just dropped a couple of cubes into each glass and swirled them.

He handed one to Thompson, looked for a place to sit and then settled onto the bed. They drank silently for a moment and then Thompson stood up and said, "I guess it's about time for bed."

Brown moved to the dresser, set his glass on it and said, "I better be going then."

Thompson looked at him as if he had said something incredibly stupid. She shook her head and said, "Who said anything about you leaving?"

It had been as simple as that. Brown had stared at her, his mind racing. In the back of his mind, he could see this causing trouble, but up front he didn't care. "Then I'll lock the door, since I'm up."

"Good. And then get over here."

"Yes ma'am. Right away."

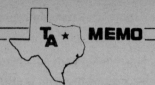

T A ★ MEMO

HISTORICAL PERSPECTIVE:

The 25th, the second full day of the siege, dawned with a cold drizzle falling. The Mexicans had been busy the night before, throwing up another earthwork just across the river and protected by the houses near it.

The second skirmish came late in the morning. Men on the south wall saw movement in front of them before a hail of cannon fire pinned them down. In La Villita, only a few hundred yards away from the Alamo, Colonel Sesma and his Mexican artillerymen were attempting to set up another cannon position. The rough wooden huts gave them too much cover and Travis realized that it had been a mistake not to burn them earlier.

As the enemy moved closer, apparently heartened because they hadn't been fired upon, they became bolder. When they were less than one-hundred yards away, the Alamo's artillery, commanded by Captain Almeron Dickinson, opened fire. They hit a church, causing the roof to collapse, smashed an earthwork firing pit and sandbagged entrances to several structures. At the same time, riflemen, most notably Davy Crockett, opened fire with their Kentucky rifles. Men from all positions in the Alamo came running, hoping to join the fight.

A dozen Mexicans fell and the rest wavered. The advance broke, with a hasty retreat, while the Texans continued to fire into the area. More Mexicans fell.

While Crockett and his boys kept the Mexicans hiding, the Alamo gates flew open and James Rose, with several friends, ran through, carrying torches. They tossed them at the nearest of the wooden buildings and then dodged back to the fort. Rose barely escaped a Mexican officer who tried to tackle him football style.

Although the best cover was burned, the Mexicans still tried to move cannons into the area. The Texans kept a steady stream of rifle fire pounding the Mexicans, wounding anyone foolish enough to be caught in the open. By noon casualties had risen so high, work failed to progress. Colonel Sesma and his men gave up, dragging their casualties out of sight.

Not much happened the rest of the afternoon. The Mexican artillery kept firing, and there was

continued maneuvering in the La Villita area, but well
outside the range of the Texas rifles. The arrival of
more Mexican troops allowed Santa Anna to place a
detachment near the roads leading to Gonzales and
Goliad in an attempt to stop Texas messengers.

During the next few hours, there were a
number of skirmishes that built morale in the Alamo.
A group of men ran out to meet a unit of Sesma's men.
In the short firefight, the Texans came out on top. More
men raided La Villita, either knocking down or burning
more of the closest buildings to increase the field of fire
from the Alamo.

Still the luck of the Alamo held. No Texans
were hurt in the skirmishes, while the Mexicans lost
several men. In fact, the worst casualty suffered by the
Texans was Bowie. He seemed to get sicker every day,
and a few men wondered if he would survive the month.

As rain began to fall, whipped by a cold north
wind, Travis met with several of the officers in his
headquarters. Travis had decided that another message
should be sent, this time to Sam Houston. Most of the
debate was over whether to send Juan Seguin, or
someone else. Travis wanted Seguin to stay because he
was a Mexican and could be helpful if there were any
more dealings with Santa Anna. Others were equally
convinced that being a Mexican was the one reason

Seguin should go. He would be able to bluff his way past any patrols he might encounter.

Travis lost, and Seguin was selected. He took his orderly and slipped out of the fort. They were challenged briefly, but posed as two old friends out after a drunk. As they closed with the Mexican patrol, they kicked their horses and sprinted past. The surprised Mexican soldiers reacted too slowly, and Seguin and his orderly escaped without injury.

Halicar, HISTORIAN
First Assistant to the Chief Archivist

TEN

The chartered 737 landed on the sod runway near the Gonzales lab, throwing up clouds of dust as the pilot fought to stop the plane. Normally he wouldn't have allowed anyone to tell him to land on an unsurfaced runway, but the airline president had told him that the Texas-American Oil Company had promised to fill the airline's total fuel needs for the next two years at current prices. That was a plum too good to pass up, even if it meant landing on a sod strip.

So, the pilot hadn't complained when he was ordered to land at Fort Worth's Meacham Field to pick up thirty pax and their luggage, crates, and equipment. He ignored the boxes that suggested arms and looked the other way as the men and women, in unmarked camouflaged uniforms, boarded his plane. He did exactly as instructed. He took off, turned north for thirty minutes, west for an hour, and then south to San Antonio, and finally back to the east. The strip was easy to find; the long, hot summer had baked it until it was almost as hard as concrete, and it was more than long enough. Takeoff would be no problem. He would not refuel there. The passengers would be gone and the cargo compartments empty.

While the unloading was supervised by the first officer, the pilot sat in the cockpit studying his high-altitude charts with a dedication that he hadn't felt since flight school. He consciously kept his eyes away from the windows. The less he saw, the better he'd like it. Of course, he also liked the position that his limited knowledge gave him. Now, as a trusted member of the airline, he would no longer have to worry about lay-offs (employee readjustments, the company called them) or about being outbid for a good route. And there was always the bonus promised for taking the flight.

Robert Brown didn't understand what was happening. Before boarding the plane, Michael Travis had briefed him in a small room outside the offices of the Cross Country News. While the other members of the team waited in the coffee shop, looking very conspicuous in their jungle fatigues, Travis talked to Brown.

He handed Brown a dispatch case and said, "First stop will be some three hours from now, a little north of the Mexican border. You'll have to switch planes before you cross, just after dark. That won't stop radar, but at least we won't have to worry about someone seeing the plane's markings."

Travis checked his notes. "You'll be on the ground for several hours before the crossing, which will give you plenty of time to unload the plane and prepare for the next leg. You'll meet one of ours there named Isaac Millsaps. He'll tell you what you need to know as well as give you a key to that case."

"Is all this really necessary?" Brown backed up and leaned against the bar set near the wall. Through the huge plate-glass window that made up one wall, he could see an empty expanse of parking lot which indicated that all air traffic was now routed through the regional airport. He approved of using Meacham, although he would have preferred something even more private.

"Probably not. But then again, it can't hurt. Any other questions?"

"None that immediately present themselves."

"Good. Anything you need to know, and don't already, will probably be answered by the documents in that case or by Millsaps." Travis checked his watch. "Your plane will leave in about thirty minutes."

Brown moved toward the door. "Okay, Travis. Catch you in the funny papers." Opening it, he stepped into the hall and looked toward the coffee shop. Near the entrance, several of his men stood staring at the 737. Brown walked toward them and said, "Let's get ready to board. Where are the others?"

McGee swept the area with a gigantic arm gesture that took in half of Fort Worth. "Hither and yon."

"Well, round them up. I'm going to supervise the loading of our equipment."

Three hours later, Brown stood in the blast furnace heat of a late July afternoon, blinking in the stinging dust of a strong westerly breeze, watching his men and women unload the equipment. They stacked it on a series of small hand-trucks while Millsaps danced around them shouting contradictory orders that they politely ignored. Millsaps directed them and the equipment to a dilapidated quonset hut near the airfield, proclaiming that they could wait inside, out of the heat, where cold drinks could be purchased in the world's oldest Coke machine. It still took dimes for bottles and not half-bucks for cans.

Millsaps had them push the hand-trucks along one edge

of the hut, supposedly so that the equipment wouldn't be damaged, and then told everyone to grab a drink and take a seat. His instructions were to give them a last-minute briefing to ensure that everyone understood the corporate mission.

While the twenty-eight mercenaries looked for places to sit, Brown walked toward a covered easel that had been placed a few feet from one end of the hut. There were four small windows with shades that Millsaps was systematically darkening. When he finished, he joined Brown at the easel, and then picked up a small phone, reached over and punched a button set on the wall and hung up. He turned back toward the mercenaries and said, "Ladies and gentlemen. May I have your attention?"

Apparently he couldn't, since everyone ignored him. One or two of the men had taken out their knives and were sharpening them. Not that they needed it, but it was a way to pass idle time. Others checked personal weapons. Some sat on the floor, their backs to the walls, and had closed their eyes for some last-minute sleep.

Millsaps noticed all that but overlooked it. He glanced at Brown who was leaning against the wall, smiling. Millsaps said, "Please. Ladies and gentlemen."

Still there was no response. Millsaps turned to Brown. "Colonel, would you please straighten out your people? I have some important things to tell them. Mr. Lewis, himself, gave me my orders."

Brown let the noise continue for a moment, watching Millsaps' futile efforts. Finally he said quietly, "All right, people, let's give this man our attention."

As if a switch had been thrown, there was silence in the hut. Every eye turned to Millsaps. He was so surprised by the sudden change that it took him a moment to recover. Regaining his composure, he said, "First, let me welcome you to the Texas-American Oil Company. I realize that you all have worked for us for several weeks, but this is going to be your first real assignment."

He let the words sink in, believing that they were impressed with the intensity of his voice. He tried to maintain eye contact with the entire group, just as his executive training seminar had taught him. He knew that the men and women were competent professionals, but as a high-ranking member of the corporation, he didn't care.

"The first thing I want to talk about is the mission, itself. I'm afraid that it is going to be slightly different than you expected. Yes, there will be a small rebel force for you to assist, as well as a dictatorial government to be thrown out. But, it's not in Africa, as you have been led to believe."

As he reached for the cloth covering the easel, Millsaps said, "If you all would move a little closer, please, we'll get on with the briefing. Please, everyone, move up." He waited until they were clustered in front of him, away from the walls and in the center of the hut.

He whipped the cloth away so that everyone could see the three-dimensional drawing of an old fort. Millsaps nodded approvingly at the startled reactions of the mercenaries. He said, "There is no mistake. The legend you see on top is correct. This is our target." As he spoke, he put the tip of the pointer under the title.

It said, simply, "THE ALAMO. 1836."

HISTORICAL PERSPECTIVE:

On the 26th, the battle changed little. Skirmishers ran out once or twice to turn minor threats. More men ran to La Villita, both for firewood and to burn huts to move the enemy lines further back. At the same time, the Texans kept shooting at the Mexicans moving around in La Villita, and they continued to inflict casualties.

On the 27th, things worsened for the men of the Alamo. The wind continued, making everyone cold and miserable. The night before had been a continuous stream of bugles, alerts, faked attacks, and periodic bombardment.

During the next few days, the siege became monotonous, the Mexicans always pushing their earthworks closer, maneuvering for better positions, and trying to tighten the ring around the Alamo. At night there were more bugles, more cannons, and more fake attacks. Santa Anna was doing everything he could think of to wear down the defenders. The weather

didn't help. The cold wind was relentless, and there
were periods of freezing drizzle.

On the 28th, Santa Anna received word that
Fannin was on the way with 200 men. Fannin had
started on the afternoon of the 26th, moving slowly
against the wind and rain. About ten miles out of Goliad
a supply wagon broke down and just as repairs to it
were completed, two more wagons fell apart.

With only one team of oxen, quite a few
cannons, wagons and powder, they worked long hours
trying to ford a river. The work was slow and
discouraging but finally <u>fin</u>ished. With daylight fading,
Fannin decided to call a halt and wait for morning.
They were still in sight of Goliad.

The next morning they found new problems
and by mid-morning had failed to move more than a
few hundred yards. It was then that the officers asked
to hold a council of war, the upshot being that they
didn't think the expedition was wise. In the end,
Fannin, the organizer, elected to ignore Travis' call for
help. He decided to abandon the men of the Alamo and
retreat to his own fort.

Later in the evening, the Texans spotted a
group of enemy soldiers moving toward the footbridge.
Colonel Juan Bringas and several of his men, out on a
scouting mission, were suddenly caught in the open.

The Texans fired, killing one and wounding two or three others. Bringas had to dive into the river to avoid being shot.

That was the first real engagement between the men of the Alamo and Santa Anna's troops. The Texans won. The victory, however, wasn't much. All it did was irritate the Mexicans.

Halicar, HISTORIAN
First Assistant to the Chief Archivist

ELEVEN

Outside the quonset hut, Mary Jo Andross and Andy Kent waited while Bob Cunningham ran into the house at the far end of the compound. He returned in a minute shaking his head. "Those tapes must be in the lab."

Kent looked across the dusty road at the airstrip. "What's with the plane?"

"How would I know?" shrugged Cunningham.

Kent turned to Andross. "Tuck say anything to you about an airplane ride?"

"Nope. He just said that he was going to Dallas to talk to the brass and that we should have some fun and try to be back Monday morning, although if we aren't, he didn't think that it would hurt."

Cunningham shook his head. "I don't think I like this."

"What's not to like? It's just an airplane."

"Come on, Mary Jo, use your head. They arrange it so that all of us are off the property and then land someone in a big fancy jet. I don't see how it can be anything but trouble."

Andross leaned against the car. "I don't see anyone."

"You never do."

Kent said. "Let's check out the buildings and if we find anything that we don't like, we'll call the sheriff. I doubt seriously if there is anything nefarious."

Cunningham pointed to the quonset hut. "Somebody has drawn the shades in there."

"Let's take a look. Mary Jo, you wait here."

"Not on your life."

The door was unlocked, and Cunningham threw it open. Inside he could see the mercenaries grouped around and listening to a man in front. Cunningham didn't wait to be invited in, but charged forward, demanding, "Who in the hell are all you people?"

Millsaps looked up in surprise. He saw three people burst into the hut, two men dressed in cut-offs and T-shirts and a woman in white shorts and a halter. His mouth worked as if he couldn't get a good breath. He wanted to shout, to chase the intruders out, but suddenly it was too late. The walls began to shimmer and pulsate, indicating that they were on their way back through time.

Holes appeared in the corrugated metal around them and expanded slowly until the walls disappeared, letting in the blinking sun and racing moon as the days and nights burned into weeks and months, and the years melted away. There were instances of cold, rain that fell but seemed to vanish before it reached the ground, and blasts of heat that tried to overwhelm. They picked up speed, or seemed to, and the days were like the flashing of a gigantic strobe that gave movement the jerky, unreal appearance of an old movie. Unconsciously Millsaps waited for everything to turn black and white because television had conditioned him to think of the past as black and white. He was surprised as the atmosphere became cleansed of dust and debris, and the colors seemed to become sharper and clearer.

In seconds they were all sitting on the damp grass in a

chilly February dawn, staring at Millsaps and waiting for him to say something. Anything. Anything that would explain the strange experience. Anything at all.

Millsaps moved to shield the front of the easel, almost as if he wanted to hide it from Andross, Cunningham, and Kent. Staring at them, he demanded, "Who the hell are you?"

Cunningham recovered first. Pushing his way to the front, he said, "I've asked you the same question. And who authorized you to use our equipment?"

"Never mind that," Millsaps sighed "My God, another woman."

Cunningham reached out and grabbed the front of Millsaps' camouflaged shirt. "Don't get side-tracked. I want to know what is going on."

From the side of the hut, or what had been the hut, Brown said, "I think we all have the right to know what's going on."

Millsaps pulled away, brushed his shirt as if it had gotten dirty, and said to Brown, "I guess we don't need to worry about security now, but I want you to watch these people."

"We're not going anywhere," Kent shot back.

"Talk to me, Millsaps," growled Brown.

Millsaps answered quietly, realizing that, even with the interruption, he finally had the full attention of the mercenaries. "There was no easy way to tell you. We couldn't say anything too early for fear there would be a leak and the Government would shut down the project and confiscate the notes and equipment.

"Further, if I had come into the room and told you that we would be making a trip through time and yes, that is exactly what we have done, you all would have laughed yourselves sick. But sitting here," Millsaps waved an arm

indicating the empty prairie, "you are more inclined to believe me.

"There isn't a whole lot to say about this," he continued. "One of our pure research projects came across time
travel by accident. At least, we think it was by accident.
But that is the purpose of such projects. All corporations
sponsor them, hoping that something useful and profitable
will result." Millsaps shook his head as if to wipe away the
thoughts. "But you really don't want to hear this."

Letting go of the pointer, he reached behind the picture
of the Alamo for a small, sealed envelope. He handed it to
Brown, who turned it over, examining the entire outside
before asking, "And what's this?"

"It's the key to your case which contains your orders.
Most of the things you were told up to this point aren't
worth the paper they were written on. They were only a
cover for this mission."

From the back someone shouted, "How much of this
horseshit are we supposed to believe?"

Another said more quietly, "Looks like all of it. How
else do you explain our being here?"

That keyed a general mumbling that grew in intensity as
more of the mercenaries joined discussions that quickly became arguments. The consensus seemed to be that the oil
company was playing some kind of elaborate joke, probably for training purposes. Only Thompson, who had been
watching him, noticed that Brown seemed to be as bewildered as the rest.

For a few moments, Millsaps said nothing, just watched
the mercenaries as they argued with each other and tried to
adjust to a concept that belonged in science fiction. After
scrutinizing each face, he said, "Ladies and gentlemen, we
are here to defend the Alamo from several thousand Mexican soldiers." He pulled another envelope from the stand

and opened it as the mercenaries began shouting at each other.

When the grumbling quieted, Cunningham spoke to the group. "I don't know what the plan is, exactly, but I can tell you, from personal experience, that this time travel horseshit, as you call it, is a fact." He pointed to Mary Jo and Kent. "With these two people and T.R.B. Tucker, we have found a method of time travel. We are now in a time different from the one we were in earlier today."

"Tell the kid to shut up."

With that, the room erupted again. It was apparent that there wasn't anything that Millsaps could do to stop the noise. Brown had drifted backward, almost outside the circle of influence, where he could rest his back against a tree and read the memos, notes, and reports that had been given to him. Millsaps waited for a lull in the noise before shouting, "Please. Let me have your attention. I'll try to explain this a little better."

But now the mercenaries weren't interested in what Millsaps had to say. They were trying to convince each other that it was a trick and that any second the walls would reappear and they would be back inside the hot metal shack sitting by the dusty sod runway. They shouted at each other, glared at each other, and demanded explanations that none of them had. Millsaps stood there, trying desperately to attract their attention.

After several minutes, the arguments seemed to run out of steam. One by one the mercenaries fell silent, looking alternately from Millsaps to Brown to the three strangers, waiting for one of them to fill in the gaps in their knowledge. Millsaps jumped into the quiet and said, "Ladies and gentlemen, there are a number of things that you'll want to know about the fort, the armies involved, and the mission. I have here a complete briefing package. The information should prove very useful."

"The only information that we're interested in is how the hell we get out of here and back home."

"Yeah. You tell us that."

"Please. I'll fill in the details. Just be patient."

"Not on your life, turkey. We want to know now."

Millsaps took a deep breath as he felt the anger building like pressure behind a weakened dam. "All right," he snapped. "I've had enough of this constant complaining. I'll get to the information that you all are interested in, but I'll do it my way."

"Just make it snappy, fella."

Millsaps turned toward the man who had spoken last, almost said something to him, and then just shook his head. Instead, he pulled his notes from the envelope and began the briefing.

"The siege of the Alamo began on February 23, 1836. There were about 150 Texans holding the fort while nearly 5000 Mexicans tried to take it away from them. The preliminaries are really unimportant. History tells us a great deal about all this, and if anyone is interested, we'll go into it privately later.

"What we have to know, what you'll want to know, is how the final battle shapes up. According to all available records, and remember that both sides were not eliminated, only one, so those records are complete, Santa Anna, the Mexican general, lays siege to the fort for twelve days, bombarding it almost continually, trying to breach the walls. He finally succeeds a couple of days from now. Late in the afternoon of March five, he launches an assault, hoping to catch the defenders unprepared. His thinking is that the fading sun will give his troops some cover. The main assault force hits the southeastern corner of the fort, near the palisade guarded by Davy Crockett. Although they take heavy casualties, they manage to climb the wall and reach the inner courtyard. Crockett's force is much too small and his men are quickly killed. With one part of the wall taken, the rest of the defense collapses as the Texans try to find some safety. They hole up in the rooms along the walls in a last-ditch effort which fails. Less than three hours after the assault begins, the fort falls. Mexican losses are nearly 1500 killed and wounded."

While Millsaps talked, Brown ripped open the envelopes he found in the briefcase, and took out the flimsy sheets. He scanned them quickly, saw that it was a precise battle plan of the final assault, including the names of battalions involved, brief biographies of the officers leading them, objectives as determined through research, and results of specific encounters between Texas forces and Mexican attackers. Brown tuned out Millsaps and slowly read the material, wondering why the Texas-American Oil Company would go to all the trouble to provide the very interesting information that had little to do with stopping the assault. Brown could immediately see where to place his men and women so that the Mexicans wouldn't be able to breach the walls.

When Brown finished, he looked up and heard Millsaps answering questions about time travel. Brown could see little point in debating the reality of time travel since they seemed to be right where Millsaps said they were. They had started in a small lab near a fairly built-up little town, and suddenly they were on open prairie where there was no sign of human life. Until there was more data, Brown figured it was useless to question Millsaps. He was more interested in the military targets and the possible gains to be realized by the corporation.

Standing by themselves, away from the mercenaries and Millsaps, were Andross, Cunningham, and Kent. Although no one had told them yet, Kent had said that it was apparent that Texas-American had tried to engineer it so that all members of Tucker's staff would be gone for a day or more to allow the corporation to use the equipment. It also explained Williamson's sudden interest in everything that they had done. He was probably back in the lab pushing the buttons. None of them had figured out exactly what was happening, but Millsaps' Alamo lecture had provided more than enough clues.

Now Millsaps was trying to explain how they had moved in time and why the building had disappeared. He said, "As I understand it, the field generated covers us like a dome. The walls and ceiling of the hut were outside the field because the energy required to move that extra unnecessary weight was so prohibitive. That is why I had you all move forward, away from the walls.

"The exact means, or rather the science involved, eludes me. Dr. Tucker tried to explain it, but he got so wound up in technicalities and four-bit scientific jargon that I couldn't follow it."

"How the hell do we get back?"

"Yeah. Providing we accept your story."

Kent stepped forward. "Normally, retrieval would be through a recall issued at the far end. In other words, Dr. Tucker would decide that it is time for the equipment to come back and, since there would be no specific mission, our recalls would not impair completion of the task. We would just be interested in what photos or tapes had been made."

Millsaps waved a hand to stop Kent and was about to speak when one of the mercenaries said, "We don't care about that. How do we get back?"

"Again, I'm lost in the jargon," said Millsaps. "I suppose that one of these young people can explain it if you want the exact details. Suffice it to say that we have been given a beacon, as Tucker calls it. Somehow it maintains a link with the transference device at the other end and once we activate the signal, we will be recalled. This gives us the added flexibility we need. We can move around in this era without marking this location as our retrieval point. The beacon can show the lab people where we are."

"Well," someone shouted, "let's punch the damned button and blast out of here."

"You can't do that," countered Millsaps, "you haven't fulfilled your contracts."

"We can still punch the button."

"Yeah, Millsaps, you best show us the beacon. If you won't, I'll bet one of those new people will."

Unconsciously, Millsaps took a step backward. He pointed behind them and said, "The beacon is stored over there, but I'm afraid that it won't do you any good. There is a coded sequence that has to be used to activate it and only I know the code. The beacon, without it, is worthless."

From the side someone said, "I'm sure we could persuade you to tell us that code."

"Probably would be easy. And if you won't, one of the new people will."

Cunningham took the floor. "I'm afraid we can't help you with that. We were asked to come up with a way to initiate retrieval from the far end, from the field. The easiest way was to build a radio transmitter that used a rather obscure frequency and then have it use a dot and dash sequence that would be broadcast continuously. The lab computers would scan for that sequence, home on it, and make the retrieval. Our only problem was to come up with a power supply that would last for centuries."

"What for?"

"Well, don't you see? The beacon travels through time like the rest of us. It will sit here for a hundred and fifty odd years. The computer won't look for the signal until after we left the future. When it finds the code, it initiates the recall, based on where the beacon is."

"Do you mean that the beacon will sit here for one-hundred and fifty years? It doesn't travel into the future more rapidly than normal time?"

"I'm afraid not."

"But then we'll all be dead when we're recalled."

"No. What happens is that we ask for the recall and then are almost immediately taken back into the future. But we won't be called back until we actually want it to happen."

One of the men sat with his head in his hands, groaning. "I don't get it."

Kent took over. "Maybe this analogy will help. It's not totally accurate, but it should clarify things. Think of it this way. We traveled from point A to point B using a train. It's a two-hour trip. When it's time to go home, we have to send a message back the way we came and that, too, is a two-hour trip. Once the message is received at the other end, they can dispatch the train. The difference is that through a time warp, we don't have to wait four hours. The instant we dispatch our message, the other end, in effect, picks it up and the vehicle for our return to the future begins the trip for us. We are basically taking a short cut. Our trip home takes minutes instead of the years it should."

Millsaps said, somewhat aghast, "You mean that the beacon just sits? It could be found and destroyed, or it could be moved. Nature could ruin it."

"We never said that it was foolproof. No one in Dallas would tell us what they wanted the beacon for. We came up with an easy way to do the task. It will work, as long as the beacon isn't destroyed. The atomic batteries should be good for five or six centuries."

"But what if someone finds it and moves it?"

"I would think," said Cunningham, "that the people on the other end would be able to figure that out. If they make the recall and come up empty, it means that the beacon has been moved. The only target they have, then, is this spot. I would imagine that they would try here. So, even if it has been moved, it's no real problem."

Before anyone could ask anything else, Brown stepped forward, waving his envelope. As the mercenaries fell silent, he said, "You know, Texas-American has provided us with an interesting problem here. I'm sure that if you take the time to think about it, you'll realize that we have a unique opportunity to see how a well-equipped, relatively small force can fare against a numerically superior enemy."

"Can the shit, Colonel. We didn't sign on for this."

"That point can be debated, if we're inclined to worry about niceties like that. The least we can do is look at the Alamo."

One of the men who was originally from Texas surprised the others by saying, "We should go help. The defenders put up such a heroic struggle and they came so close to winning that they deserve anything we can do for them."

"Oh, horseshit."

"Horseshit, yourself," said the Texan. "This is the kind of thing that you dream about. The great battles you missed because you were born at the wrong time. The things that you could . . ." He stopped, realizing that he had gone farther than intended.

Brown filled the gap by saying, "There is no reason not to at least take a look at the place. If anything has been misrepresented to us, we can always ride back here and punch out. I'm for looking it over."

The Texan chimed in. "Me too. At least take a look."

That stirred another debate. Half the force wanted no part of a war in Texas in 1836, while the others felt that it would do no harm to survey the situation and make a decision based on that. Millsaps let the debate go without saying a word. Another management seminar he had attended had taught him that it was sometimes necessary to let the troops argue and complain among themselves so that they would be ready to get back to the job. He knew that there was really very little they could do about the situation, and there was even less he could do to stop the discussion. He was counting on their spirit of adventure.

Millsaps glanced at his watch and was only mildly surprised to see that it was still set for the afternoon of the day they had left the future. He knew that Williamson was sitting in the lab, preparing to send the horses and supplies. They would arrive about three-hundred yards away, if the calculations were correct. Williamson had been afraid to set them down closer, not knowing what the effects would be as they arrived.

It was too bad that Texas-American had to spend the money to send the horses, but it was believed that horses in war-torn Texas would be at a premium, so they had underwritten the cost. The rest of the supplies, food, and ammunition were things that couldn't be bought in Texas in 1836, and so the budget had been expanded to include them.

As the debate slowed, Millsaps checked the sun. If the figures were right, it was about 9:00 in the morning. It was time to get moving so that they could get to the Alamo under the cover of darkness. Millsaps moved closer to Brown and said, "Any time you would like to get your people ready to head out . . ."

Brown nodded, folded his envelope, and buttoned it into one of the pockets of his fatigue jacket. He had decided that they would go to the Alamo. He knew his people well enough to know that they would follow his decision. There were things that he would never be able to convince them to do, and a lot of things he would never try to persuade them to do, but he had, during the training, earned their respect. He could ask them to follow him without providing a lengthy explanation of the request.

He glanced at the new people. Although their dress was acceptable for the future, Brown didn't think it would pass in 1836 Texas. The woman, in her shorts and halter, looked almost as if she were wearing only undergarments. The two men were a little more appropriately dressed, but the cut-offs would have to be replaced. Brown had had the foresight to demand an extra set of uniforms for everyone. Now that he knew the mission would last less than a week, he could ask his people to give up some of their extra clothes. And he would have to find weapons for them.

He said to Cunningham, Kent, and Andross, "I'm getting you people some better clothes. I suppose you know what we're supposed to do."

"We can figure it out," said Kent.

"Then you can understand why I have to ask what kind of experience you have for this sort of thing."

Kent laughed. "I doubt if anyone has any experience at this. However, I assume you mean military. I spent four years flying helicopters for the Army, including a year in Vietnam. I've spent the last few years in the Air Force Reserve. I can shoot well with a handgun, rifle, and a variety of larger weapons, including a Vulcan cannon."

Cunningham said, "And I was a Marine for a couple of years and did one tour. I'm also in the Air Force Reserve. I can field, strip, clean, and repair practically any small arms made in the world today, or rather in the future. I'm trained in hand-to-hand combat and the use of the bayonet."

"And you?" Brown said to Andross.

"I'm afraid I don't know much about guns, except what I've seen on TV. But I'm trained in first aid, including CPR. I can probably help the doctor in some way."

"I don't think they have a doctor at the Alamo. You might be able to assist my two medics," said Brown.

"Okay."

Millsaps interrupted. "Colonel Brown, we must get going."

Brown turned away from the newest members of the team and said, "If there are no objections, let's go take a look at the Alamo."

There was a momentary silence and then someone said, "Why the hell not?" and no one could think of a good answer to that. Without a word, Millsaps started toward the small valley screened by trees, where the horses were supposed to have materialized, afraid that they wouldn't be there. He heard a whinny and looked back at the mercenaries, gesturing them forward.

When Brown saw the horses, he said to himself, "That explains why they insisted on the riding." He pointed and said, "Some of you grab the equipment."

They spent the next hour saddling the horses and packing the equipment, while Millsaps studied his maps and tried to hurry them. When they were ready, Millsaps pointed to the hills in the west and said, "Over there, somewhere, is the road leading to San Antonio. It shouldn't be hard to find."

Brown shrugged. "Fine." He turned to the men and women. "Mount up." As an afterthought, he ordered, "Bugler, sound 'Boots and Saddles'."

"We don't have a bugler."

"Then hum it, for Christ's sake."

HISTORICAL PERSPECTIVE

The siege on February 29 didn't change, but the weather lightened and the wind stopped; still the Mexicans continued to maneuver. The men in the Alamo would have been excited if they had known that much of the maneuvering was caused by the belief that Fannin was coming. Santa Anna still hadn't learned the truth, and the Texans, at least part of them, thought that help would arrive soon.

The only real change was new earthworks erected closer to the walls. Several Mexican battalions changed position during the day, some of them ending where they had started. It was all designed to bewilder the men holed up in the Alamo, to prevent Fannin from reaching them, and to stop the Texans from escaping.

Late on February 29, James Butler Bonham rode into Goliad, went straight to Fannin's headquarters to give him the note written by Travis. Fannin read it and then refused to budge. Frank Johnson, who had led many of the Alamo's garrison

104

away on the Matamores expedition, also arrived and
told of the Mexican slaughter of the Texans. That
underscored Fannin's decision. Fannin told Bonham to
stay, but Bonham refused. He had to find help.

Bonham took off for Gonzales only to find
the town empty. But he learned that a small group of
men had ridden to the Alamo the day before. Bonham
ran into another of Travis' messengers who had tried
to get back to the Alamo only to find the roads blocked
by Mexican cavalry. He told Bonham that he should go
to San Felipe, where an army was forming. Bonham
again refused, claiming that he had to try to report to
Travis, even if he had failed.

Halicar, HISTORIAN
First Assistant to the Chief Archivist

TWELVE

Tucker was in an ugly mood. When he returned from Dallas, he found that Williamson had been playing with the equipment. He had checked the power curves and consumption figures and learned that a couple of substantial loads had been sent more than a century into the past. And Williamson could not be reached for comment. It was obvious that the briefing in Dallas had been a ruse to get him out of the lab.

Cunningham, Kent, and Andross had not returned from their weekend off, and, while Tucker didn't care about that, he was concerned because he hadn't heard from them. Normally, when one of them was going to be late returning, he or she called, primarily to make sure that a critical experiment wasn't scheduled. It was a courtesy they showed each other.

And to make it worse, the rabbit died.

Not only the rabbit, but two of the guinea pigs, one white rat, and one chimpanzee. And a number of the other test animals were sick.

In the two days that Tucker had been back, he thought he had found the reason for it. He didn't like making a report with so little data, but after the glowing presentation he had given in Dallas, at Williamson's insistence, Tucker felt that he should make Travis aware of the problems.

Tucker sat in his green chair and lit a cigar. He tossed the match at the ashtray, watched it hit the desk and bounce once, landing right where he wanted it. When the call went through, he announced, "I think we may have a problem."

"What sort of problem?" asked Travis.

"Possibly an insurmountable one," Tucker replied. "I mentioned Friday that the rabbit hadn't traveled well and was concerned about it. It died. And so have others."

"Other rabbits?"

"Other test animals. After the rabbit died, I ran other tests with rats, guinea pigs, and chimpanzees. Some lived, some died. I can't be positive with so little data, but I've worked out a theory, of sorts, that seems to make sense. Simply stated, I think time killed them. In a sense, we killed them, but basically, it was time."

"I think you're going to have to explain that more fully," said Travis, "because I don't have the slightest notion of what you're talking about."

"I ran a number of tests," replied Tucker. "In those where the test animal remained in the past for only a few seconds or minutes, little or no ill effects were observed. In those in which the test animal remained behind for longer periods, say several minutes to an hour or so, the returned animals showed signs ranging from fatigue to physical and nervous exhaustion. Those animals remaining much over an hour, say an hour and a half to three hours, exhibited symptoms varying from acute distress to death."

"Are you telling me that if we send someone back, he'll die?" asked Travis hoarsely, sensing his own and Lewis' dreams of unlimited wealth and power crumbling.

"Not at all," Tucker answered. "Recording equipment we sent back with the animals, movie cameras, EEG and EKG recorders, that sort of thing, all indicated the animals did fine until we tried to retrieve them. When we put them into the return phase of the transfer field, they went into acute distress. Tachycardia arrythmia, shock, cardio-respiratory failure, hepatic failure, renal failure, severe nervous trauma, the whole works. The longer they'd stayed in the past, the more complete the deterioration. Those remaining in the past the longest suffered complete internal life support systems breakdown and showed marked tissue damage in autopsy."

"I still don't understand," said Travis. "Are you telling me that if we send someone back, we'll kill him?"

"Not if we send him back. Only if we try to bring him back, or rather forward. We can send anyone or anything we want, provided we have sufficient electrical power, to any point or any time in the past and keep them there for as long as we wish. We'll kill them only when we try to bring them back to the present. That is, we'll kill them if they stay in the past for more than a few minutes or hours. Certainly death would result after a few hours of time-traveling. I cannot be sure yet at what point brain or irreparable tissue damage would occur, but it would probably be after only minutes, certainly less than an hour."

"Do you have any idea why the amount of time spent in the past makes such a difference?"

"Dozens. And it may not make any difference. We won't know that for sure until we've had a chance to really study the long-term effects on the test animals. They seem perfectly healthy now, the short-timers I mean, but it's quite impossible to second-guess what effects might show up five or ten or twenty years down the road."

"But you believe the deterioration is caused by the process of returning the subjects to the present, and not by the initial trip into the past, itself?"

"Deterioration is caused or accelerated by it. For practical purposes, there are no immediate, visible effects as long as the subjects remain in the past."

"I see. And what is your best guess for the cause behind the deterioration? Surely it's not just a matter of time?"

"As I said, there are dozens of possibilities. In a simple sense, it may be that bringing the subjects forward in time accelerates the aging process in some as-yet-unknown way. More likely, I think, and keep in mind that this is just a theory and should not necessarily be given more credence than any of the other theories, it may be a matter of cellular displacement, or rather, replacement."

"What do you mean by that?"

"The human body is a constantly growing, changing thing. All the cells in the body, with very few exceptions, replace themselves with new ones every few days. The same is true of most animals.

"Thus, if the test subject remains in the past for several hours or a few days, the body we retrieve from the past is not the same one we sent into the past. It is very nearly the same in appearance and function, but not precisely so."

"And that could make a difference?"

"Most definitely. The key to the functioning of the Trans-Spatio-Temporal Matter Transference Field is the ability of the computer-generated induction plasma to precisely discriminate between various time point locators and matter event horizons. Without precise discrimination, the random quarks interacting with the charmed quarks produce an electro-magnetic meson interference field evoking a nonsequitur informational input, thus negating target or transfer object lock-on."

Travis held the phone away from his head momentarily

and stared at it. "What does that mean in English, Dr. Tucker?"

"What? Oh, yes. Sorry. Well, I'll try." Tucker exhaled slowly, mustering his patience for dealing with the non-scientific mind, and organizing his thoughts.

"The system works," Tucker explained, "only because it can have a precise one-to-one mapping on a space-time coordinate model, of the precise, actual location of a person, place, thing, or time, in the actually existing space-time continuum. This is true for the time factor down to a measure of nanoseconds, with a scattering error of plus or minus point zero five, and for the matter/distance factors, all the way down to the subatomic level, usually expressed in angstroms times powers of ten.

"Within certain prescribed limits, the system can initiate a value judgment and make allowances for data that do not precisely fit with the known or expected norms; however, this discrimination window has exceedingly narrow limits. If it did not, the system could not function at all.

"It is my theory that with the relentless progression of real-time, that is, the passage of time as subjectively measured by the test subject while in the past, the attendant changes in tissue structure, produced by the efforts of the body to renew and maintain itself, result in the mapping relationship of the computer-generated model to the real-existing locators and event horizons, falling outside the tolerance limits of the window.

"When such a set of circumstances arises, the system compensates as best it can but cannot compensate precisely, because the real-data no longer fits with the original input data in the computer mode. It is not a question of the data in the model being inaccurate. It is the real object which has undergone change, not the model. Perhaps in time the problem can be overcome, but at present, the system simply isn't sophisticated enough to foresee all the possible modifications of cellular structure occurring throughout so complex an organism as a human body, or even a rabbit, and then second-guess the body to the extent of making only those changes in the mapping relationship of the model to the real body as have actually occurred in the organism itself.

"In my opinion, it will take a major breakthrough in scientific technology before this problem can be corrected. If ever. Even given the exponential rate of present technological advancement, I do not foresee the problem being overcome in the next several decades. Perhaps not even in the next century.

"In the meantime, however, we will have to content ourselves with the making of sound, film, and video recordings of history. At present, the difficulties involved in a safe return make the prospect of doing any real time traveling just too dangerous."

Both men were silent for a moment, Tucker having exhausted all the arguments that needed to be said against a human attempting time travel, Travis organizing his thoughts and digesting what the scientific genius had told him. Then Travis spoke.

"Why aren't inanimate objects affected?"

"Their molecular structure is fairly constant. We have had some equipment develop indications of the beginnings of oxidation, that is, rust, but this has been very slight. Inanimate objects do not change their structure with the same frequency as animate objects."

"But what about film in a camera, for instance? Surely it changes structure when an object is photographed?"

"It's not the same thing. True, there are ultimately changes in appearance, but halides of silver remain halides of silver. The clustering of the fine black silver particles of the silver bromide or silver chloride emulsion does not occur until the film is developed. Only then is the negative produced."

"All right, I think I understand this now. It isn't safe to retrieve a human or an animal who has remained very long in the past because the cells in its body have changed, and the system cannot compensate for the change. But that still doesn't tell me exactly what kills them."

"I'm sorry," said Tucker. "I thought you understood. The system cannot precisely match up actually existing structures in the changed body to the original model of those structures, but it does its best to compensate for the discrepancy. It does so in the only way it knows how. By bringing back only those tiny bits of matter that it can match up within reasonable tolerances. That's what accounts for the apparent tissue damage.

"It isn't really tissue damage, of course, because the tissue hasn't been damaged or destroyed.

"It's simply been left behind."

"So anyone we send back lives, as long as we don't try to retrieve them?"

"Yes."

"And if we do, they die?"

"Yes."

Good, thought Travis. Very good indeed.

THIRTEEN

After fifteen hours of hard riding, the mercenaries were crouched in the darkness on a hillside near the Alamo. Brown and two of his men crawled to the military crest of the hill, near a giant bush, where they could see most of San Antonio, the river, and the Mexican forces near the old fort.

"How in the hell are we supposed to get down there with the whole Goddamn Mexican army surrounding the place?" said Waters.

"Well, Tom," said Brown, scratching his beard, "I sort of figured on riding in the front gate, but it looks like we'll have to follow this dry stream bed to La Villita and break left toward the gate on the south wall. Providing Millsaps' information is right."

"That doesn't tell me what we're going to do about the Mexican army."

Thompson spoke. "It also doesn't tell us how we're going to let the Texans know we're friendly so they don't shoot the hell out of us."

Brown snapped off his pen light and folded the map. "That shouldn't be much of a problem. The Texans will know we're friendly because the Mexicans will be trying to shoot the hell out of us."

"Terrific."

They crawled down the hillside, stood up, and moved back to their horses. Brown stuffed the map in his saddle bag and turned back to Waters. "Go find Millsaps and tell him to get his corporate butt up here."

Robert Jones stepped out of the inky-black shadows. "Sir, there's a cavalry patrol about four-hundred yards off to our right, moving this way slowly. Sewell spotted them with his starlight scope."

"Then I suggest we get the hell out of here. Tell everyone to mount up, and then find out what's keeping Waters and that damned historian."

Waters rushed uphill, dragging Millsaps by the sleeve.

"Okay, big mouth," said Brown. "What do your notes have to say about how we're supposed to get into the fort?"

"Most of the references are pretty vague. Couriers like Bonham rode in and out all the time, but no mention is made of passwords or signals."

"Thanks a lot."

Joe Hawkins came back up the hill, leading his horse. "Sir, those Mexicans are getting awfully close."

"All right. All right. I guess the only thing to do is try riding into the place. Have everyone draw their pistols. We don't want to give away any military secrets by using the automatic weapons yet, or have the Texans think the entire Mexican army is attacking at once. Put those new people and Millsaps in the middle of the column, and detail one of the men to watch out for them. Move out slowly and quietly. You take the point, Hawkins."

They moved down off the hill and into the dry creek bed. The horses strung out in a long, well-spaced line, picking their way cautiously in the poor light that filtered down from the quarter moon through the broken, stratified cumulus clouds.

Then, seemingly from nowhere, two men loomed out of the darkness in front of Hawkins. He jumped slightly to one side, nearly falling out of the saddle, as he tried to swing his pistol toward the men.

"I wouldn't shoot that thing if I was you, mister," said the nearest man. "Less of course you want to bring all of El Presidente's cavalry riding down on top of us."

"Who the hell are you?" hissed Hawkins.

"Name's Sutherland. Sort of figured on asking you the same question."

Hawkins ignored that and gestured toward the other man. "Who's he?"

"John Smith. Colonel Travis sent us to find reinforcements."

"Well, you found us. We're here."

"I can see, mister. But you still haven't told me who you are."

"Reinforcements from Gonzales."

Brown rode up then. "What's the delay, Hawkins?" He stared into the gloom. "Who are these people?"

There was a moment of silence, and then a musket shot from the rear.

"Let's scram," said Sutherland.

"Where to?"

"The Alamo, of course. Unless you're figuring on fighting the Mexicans out here in the open."

"Lead the way," said Brown.

Sutherland swung up on his horse. "Follow me."

There were several more musket shots and one or two answering pistol shots. To the rear, the growing bedlam suggested that the Mexicans were closing rapidly. "Move out," yelled Brown. Sutherland and Smith took off at a gallop, and the rest followed, including a troop of Mexicans.

For a moment, it looked good. Then, out of the blackness to the right, another troop of Mexican cavalry appeared, riding hard to cut off Brown and his mercenaries.

"Oh hell," said Brown. "Skirmish line right and left. Fire at fifty yards."

Guns blazing, the party charged through the startled Mexicans and rode hard for the Alamo. A hundred yards from the fort, a dozen shots rang out from the wall.

"Don't shoot, you stupid bastards," yelled Sutherland. "It's me and Smith with reinforcements."

Brown brought his horse up short, by the wall, leaped off, took two running steps to re-gain his balance, and whirled, firing at the Mexicans. The nearest mercenaries dismounted. Crouching behind their horses, they covered the rest until they were safely inside the gate. From the parapet, Texans poured a stream of lead balls toward the cavalry, firing quickly by picking up fresh rifles, rather than reloading. The pursuit broke abruptly when someone fired a cannon.

With the Mexicans galloping out of range, Sutherland, leaning against the wall near Brown, said, "That's quite a pistol you got there. How do you load it so fast?"

"Magazine feed," said Brown. "It holds fourteen rounds."

Sutherland looked at him in obvious disbelief. "Ain't got that many barrels."

As they moved through the gate, there was an enormous cheer. A dozen men ran from the chapel and began slapping the mercenaries on the shoulders and pumping their hands.

Waters turned to Brown. "Friendly bunch, aren't they?"

Sutherland pointed to a man in a dark coat and white trousers who had left a building on the west wall. As he walked toward them, he was buckling on a sword. "Yonder comes Colonel Travis. You'll be wanting to talk to him."

The walls emptied of men as the defenders swarmed into the plaza, slapping first the mercenaries and then each other on the back. The man with the sword pointed to a group of Texans.

"You men get back to your posts."

Brown came to rigid attention and offered a crisp salute. "Lieutenant Colonel Robert Brown and thirty-two volunteers reporting for duty."

Travis made a wave of his hand approximating a salute. Over the cheering, Brown could barely hear him say, "Colonel William Barret Travis, Officer Commanding."

FOURTEEN

It took Travis several minutes to chase the guards back to
their posts. Everyone wanted to meet the reinforcements.
Travis finally gave up, telling John Baugh, the adjutant, to
see about finding quarters for the new arrivals. He pointed
to the headquarters set on the west wall and asked Brown
to accompany him.

As they moved away from the shouting group, Travis
said, "Those men should be sleeping. We've gotten very
little the last week or so."

"Sometimes you just have to let them get it out of their
systems."

Travis stopped at the bank of the brook that bordered the
rooms built inside the west wall to let Brown use the tiny
footbridge first. "I don't care what they do," said Travis,
"as long as it doesn't impair their ability to fight."

"You can't ask for more than that."

"Not really. Besides, they're mostly volunteers." Travis
opened a door and held out a hand to indicate the way.

"Have a seat, Colonel. I'll light a couple of lamps."

"Thanks." Brown sat down and glanced around the room, surprised that a fat lamp could give off so much light.

Travis fell into the chair on the opposite side of the table, arched his back to loosen the stiff muscles, and said, "Tell me about yourself, Colonel."

"Not much to tell, really. I've soldiered in a number of small wars, commanded troops in a couple of them, and planned strategy in one or two."

"Anything I have heard of?"

"Probably not. Most of it was in southeast Asia. And I did a few things in southern Africa."

"I can't tell you how happy we are that you and your men made it in. Any more of you coming?"

"Not from Gonzales." Brown waved toward the door. "Your own people will tell you that. I think most went to find Houston."

Travis nodded. "I suppose so." He hesitated, pulling at a splinter on the rough wooden table. "How much powder did you bring? We're running short."

"Colonel, I think there is something I should tell you." Brown tried to think of a good way to explain it. He looked around the small, dirty room. It wasn't much to look at. There was an adobe floor and adobe walls. Near the door was one window with the disintegrating wooden shutters closed. The only furniture was the table, three chairs, and something that looked like an end table. Two fat lamps bubbled on the wall, sending black smoke toward the ceiling. The room had a dirty smell to it, as if someone had tried to sweep it, but had only succeeded in stirring up the dust. Brown leaned forward, his elbows on the table. "Our weapons aren't compatible. Mine use a cartridge made of a primer and powder and a bullet. It's all one unit. They won't work in your weapons."

Travis sat staring at Brown. "I don't quite understand."

"The weapons we brought are automatics." Brown pulled one of the pistols from its holster and placed it on the table. He released the magazine and held it up. Slowly he extracted several of the cartridges, setting them on their bottoms on the table. "We use these rather than powder and ball. It lets us reload faster and makes it possible for us to use more than one round before we have to reload." Brown realized that he sounded as if he was lecturing a rather slow child.

"Use these instead of powder?" Travis picked up one and looked at it.

"It's a new invention. They haven't been out very long. Came from the Colt Firearms Company." Brown knew that the lie was flimsy, but it should cover the event for history. Samuel Colt had developed a revolver some time in 1835. The survivors of the battle might later talk of the fantastic weapons Brown and his people had, but now there would be a reason for them.

"All right." Travis stood and moved to the window. He turned back toward Brown. "I think the best place for you and your people will be the northern edge of the east wall. We're pretty weak there."

"If I might make a suggestion, Colonel, why not switch some of the other men over there and let me defend the south wall? With that open area near the chapel, you're going to need a strong force and, with our automatic weapons, it's like having another fifty or sixty men."

For a moment Travis considered telling Brown that he would fight where he was told to, but then thought better of it. The cartridges on the table and the strange pistol that Brown carried suggested that Brown might have brought something worth a lot more than the thirty-two people with him. He might have brought the means with which to win the battle. Travis wasn't sure how good these new-fangled weapons were, but he had enough military acumen to say nothing until he was sure of their value. He opened the door for Brown.

"You're probably tired. I'll show you where your men are to be quartered and we'll discuss this in the morning."

Brown was surprised as they stepped outside. It was now cold and there were high thin clouds rushing past the moon. Travis turned to the north.

"The officers are quartered here. Your men are across the plaza."

"I'd prefer to stay with my people."

Travis shrugged. "Suit yourself, but the barracks aren't quite as comfortable as the officers' area. Not that it makes that much difference."

They walked across the courtyard. A number of small fires were blazing under the protection of the walls. Knots of men slept near the fires, preferring to be outside, rather than be crowded together into dirty rooms. There was little noise until a bugle call sounded outside the walls, followed by several shouts that quickly died.

Travis stopped to listen. "That'll be nothing to worry about. The Mexicans hope that we'll rouse the garrison. Santa Anna figures that interrupted sleep is the same as no sleep. We've gotten pretty good at ignoring him."

"That could be dangerous," said Brown.

"Could be, but really isn't. He doesn't have enough men in Bexar yet. Our scouts report that the majority of his army is still three or four days' march from here."

Travis stopped outside a door. "Your people are in here. In the morning, we will talk some more about strategy and troop placement."

"I'll see you then, Colonel."

Brown watched Travis walk back to his headquarters before opening the barracks door. The room was big and surprisingly well-lighted. Lamps from a dozen places threw dancing patterns on the walls and supplemented several battery-powered lanterns the mercenaries had brought. Most of the men sat in a circle on the floor with blankets spread among them. They were cleaning and oiling their weapons.

"Where's Thompson?" asked Brown.

Waters looked up and shrugged. "She went outside a few minutes ago."

"And no one went with her?"

"Why should they? We're among friends here."

Brown took a deep breath. "I warned everyone to stick together until we had a better feel for this thing. Now you let one of our people go roaming around like it's a picnic in the park. Oh, shit. Just forget it. I'll find her." Brown spun and slammed the door on his way out.

For a moment he stood there, looking first to the south wall and then to the north, trying to figure out which way Thompson would have gone. He finally opted to check the north side first, since they had entered the fort from the south. If nothing else, it would give him a chance to see those fortifications, the attack approaches, and the fields of fire of the cannon, something that he wanted to do, anyway.

FIFTEEN

Thompson had been bothered by the whole project from the moment Millsaps had told them exactly what their mission was supposed to be. She had not had much of a chance to reflect upon it because they had moved so fast from the moment of their arrival to the time they had ridden into the fort. She climbed the dirt ramp that had been built as a cannon emplacement. After reaching the top she was surprised to find no one there. A small pyramid of cannon balls stood at one side, and there were a couple of barrels of powder, but no one to load and fire the weapon. If the Mexicans were to attack now, they could get across the open ground before the Texans could respond. But, that wouldn't happen, she knew, because they had had the whole history of the battle outlined for them by Millsaps.

The night breeze stiffened, and Thompson buttoned her jacket as she stared. There were only a few dull spots of light in the distance, apparently Mexican fires. Overhead were most of the same stars that she had seen from Saigon just before Tet, and she realized that both Tet and the Battle of the Alamo took place about the same time of year.

But what most impressed her were the darkness and silence. There had been no noise since the bugle call and shouts a few minutes earlier. Behind her was the sound of a single cow, but that was all. She moved to the left, putting one hand on the rough-cut logs that protected part of the cannon emplacement. To the east was old San Antonio, but even that was dark and quiet. The Mexican officers had given up on the cantina girls and gone back to their units. The town was no more than a dark smudge against a darker background.

At a sound behind her, she turned and heard Brown say, "There you are, Jessie."

"Bob?"

"What are you doing up here?"

"Asking myself that same question. I've been trying to sort it all out, trying to figure out what all this means."

Brown leaned against the cannon barrel. "Sort of deep thoughts, aren't they?"

"You know what I mean," she said.

"Why don't you tell me?"

Thompson turned to the north approach so that her back was to Brown. "Have you thought about what it means to change history? What it does to our future? I mean, men who are supposed to die in a few days, won't; others who are supposed to live will probably be killed by us. The battle that was once lost will be won, and the war will take a whole different turn."

"So?"

"So? So? Is that all you can say? Haven't you thought about this at all?"

Brown shook his head. "I can't say that I have."

"All right, then, I'll tell you a few things I have thought about. First, the world we go back to won't be the same as the one we left. The boundaries of Mexico and the United States will be different, if old H. Perot Lewis has his way."

"I can't see where that will affect us greatly."

Thompson turned to face him. "But it will mean that any part of history can be changed. Maybe Lewis won't like the outcome of World War II, so he fixes it. The power that this gives him is limited only by his imagination."

Brown rubbed his eyes. "No. I don't suppose we can rely on Lewis to take the good of the human race into consideration."

"Not when his first plan is to change history." Thompson paused.

In the silence, Brown's mind raced. He knew something of the history of the battle even before Millsaps had briefed them. He knew that thirty-three men from Gonzales had arrived on March first, and that had happened. What he hadn't known was that he would lead them. He suddenly realized that there should be another thirty-three men hiding somewhere. Either that or, even with their help, the Alamo would still fall.

"We don't know that history can be changed," said Brown. "The history books talk about thirty-three men riding into the fort on this date. Obviously, we're it."

Thompson slapped at the barrel of the cannon. "Then that means we will all die when the Mexicans storm the fort."

"Supposedly. But I don't see how they can get in, if we know at what point the assault will take place and if we use all our weapons. Thirty automatic weapons, backed by a couple of recoilless rifles and mortars, ought to be able to break up anything the Mexicans can throw at us. Hell, we can probably add more Texans to defend the south wall so that our force there is unbeatable."

"You're talking as if you want to win."

"Christ, Jessie. What's wrong with you?" Brown

sounded amazed. "Of course I want to win. We have to. Or die. Our fate is tied to that of the Alamo."

She stepped closer to him. "Then let's get out. We can tell old H. Perot anything. He'll never know."

For a moment Brown was tempted. He was sure they could threaten Millsaps into backing their story and creating no problems. Brown had taken a contract to defend the Alamo, even if he didn't know that it was to be the Alamo when he signed the contract, and he couldn't, with a clear conscience, break his word. Besides, he had already told Colonel Travis that he would help. He felt committed. There might be some interesting legal ramifications here. But, even so, even though he was dealing with men who had died decades before his birth, Brown couldn't abandon them.

Quietly he said, "No, Jessie. We can't just leave."

"Well, why the hell not?" she demanded.

"Because I said that we would stay and fight, and I won't break my word."

"Oh, shit. You're probably the only man from our time with such a ridiculous sense of honor. No one bothers with such commitments any more."

"I won't abandon these men to die when I know I can help."

"But they're already dead."

"Not now, they aren't. I have the ability to save them for awhile. Maybe that's it. Right now I don't know." Brown patted a pocket, searching for a cigar and then remembered that he was standing on a rather exposed part of the fort. He let his hand drop as he said, "A doctor tries like hell to save a life, even though he knows that he is eventually going to lose it. I guess I feel the same way."

She knew that she wasn't going to change his mind, at least not easily. "Well, think about what I've said. The one thing that we can't do is give Lewis the power that our victory here will achieve."

"No, I suppose we can't." He looked toward the barracks. "We'd better head back. I'm sure that Travis is going to raise holy hell tomorrow when he discovers that three of my men are women."

As they walked down the dirt ramp, Jessie asked, "What are you going to do about that?"

"Prove that you're a better soldier than any of his men."

"That could be interesting."

SIXTEEN

No one bothered to wake them in the morning. The sun was already high when Brown left his quarters. He stepped through the door and looked around slowly, surprised that the Alamo was so big. Night had hidden its size. The central courtyard covered at least three acres. Most of the walls were eight feet high and three feet thick. Slowly he moved toward the south, along the front of the two-story building that housed the hospital. He stopped at the corner to look at the chapel. It didn't really resemble the old adobe structure that stood in modern, downtown San Antonio. He knew that historians had rebuilt it so that it looked as they supposed it did when the Franciscans finished it in the middle of the eighteenth century.

A man wearing buckskins walked up to him. "You with the fellas that arrived last night?"

"Yes."

"Glad you're here."

Brown turned in a slow circle, looking at the fort. "I'm not real sure that I am."

The man laughed. "Name's Darst."

Brown held out his hand. "Brown."

"Glad to meet ya. I'm down from . . ."

Several distant booms stopped him. Darst glanced toward the log palisade that linked the chapel with the rest of the south wall. He knew the battery firing was hidden among the flimsy wooden shacks of La Villita. "Sounds like Santa Anna started the cannonade again."

When Brown didn't hear the explosions of the shells, he was momentarily mystified but then remembered that exploding cannon shells were not in common use in that time period. Most cannons fired either solid balls that were supposed to smash walls, or grapeshot, which was like a giant shotgun, designed to smash advancing troops. Brown headed for the southwest corner where the 18-pounder, the biggest of the Alamo's cannons, was sited. Darst followed behind him, not saying a word.

From the cannon emplacement, Brown could see the breastwork that had been thrown up to protect the Mexicans. There were already two others there staring at the enemy but not moving to load their own weapons. On the parapet next to the 18-pounder were a number of other men. Brown turned to the closest man and asked, "Why don't you return fire?"

The man hitchhiked a thumb over his shoulder toward the one man who was wearing a uniform of dark blue with red piping. "Cap'n Dickinson won't let us. Colonel Travis ordered us to save our powder."

"I don't suppose he would mind if some of my boys took out that battery with our weapons?"

"I don't suppose he would," answered Darst.

Another volley was fired and everyone dived for cover as the balls thudded harmlessly against the thick walls. Then from across the river, near the outskirts of San Antonio, another battery opened fire.

Brown, crouching near the 18-pounder, saw Waters standing at the base of the emplacement. He shouted down to him. "Tom, get Dennison and Wolfe and one of the 90-millimeter recoilless rifles up here. Bring a couple of snipers and we'll see if we can knock off some of this nonsense right now."

"Yes, sir."

Farther to the north a third Mexican battery opened fire. Its shots were echoed by the first two. There was another scramble for cover as one of the balls cleared the west wall and hit the second floor of the hospital, sending a shower of stone over the inner courtyard. Two or three men were clipped by the flying rock, but no one was hurt.

In less than five minutes Waters was back, helping Dennison and Wolfe carry the lightweight paratrooper weapon and its ammo up the dirt ramp. They set it next to the 18-pounder, sighted, guessed at the range, and turned to Brown. He nodded, and they fired.

The shot was short and slightly wide. It had hit one of the shacks, the 90 mm high explosive shell destroying it in a cloud of swirling debris that slowly rained back to earth.

"I don't know what you hit," shouted Dickinson, "but it blowed up real good."

The Mexicans ignored the return fire and touched off another volley.

Dennison changed the angle of the weapon, added to the elevation, and waited while Wolfe reloaded. They didn't wait for Brown's permission, but fired again. This time they hit the earthen breastwork that protected the Mexicans. They lost sight of the target in the fog of dirt that was created. Off to their right was a burst of cheering.

"Colonel Brown," said Dickinson, "That's some kinda cannon you boys got there. Does it always blow up like that?"

"Not always," said Brown. "You should see a flechette round."

When the dust cleared, the Mexicans and their cannons were still intact. Again Wolfe reloaded. As Dennison fired, Robert Crossman and James McGee crawled up to Brown.

"What do you want us to do, Colonel?"

Brown peeked over the wall. "See that battery, centered between those two buildings, the one that has half a wall in front of it, and some kind of tree on the left side of the yard?"

"Yes, sir." McGee nodded.

"All right. Any minute now there are going to be several Mexicans sprinting out of there. Dennison has the range."

"About 600 meters."

"Right." Brown scrunched down, his back against the wall and his head below the top. He squinted in the late morning sun. "Take out as many as you can."

Dennison said, "We're ready again."

"McGee, you and Crossman get in position... Any time."

Dennison fired, putting the shell between two of the Mexican cannons. Chunks of hot metal flew everywhere, while the cannoneers scrambled desperately to find cover. Both McGee and Crossman fired rapidly. Four Mexicans fell. One was dragged to the cover of the building but no one tried to retrieve the other three.

The cheering erupted again. Brown looked at Dickinson who was applauding happily. He had wanted to be able to take out at least one Mexican battery. Below the artillery command post, a number of men were jumping up and down and slapping each other on the back. One of them shouted up to Brown, "God damn, that was beautiful. Just beautiful."

Colonel Travis came galloping across the courtyard, waving a hand, and shouting, "Who gave you people permission to fire?" He skidded to a halt as Brown came down the ramp to meet him.

"No one, Colonel. We had a good target of opportunity."

"Damn it, Brown. We've got to conserve our powder. We don't have that much. I told you that last night, and I want it clearly understood that only I will order the firing of the weapons."

Brown closed his eyes for a moment. "Those were my men who fired, and we were using ammo that we brought with us. We have all that we're going to need and you already know it's a type you can't use, so there is no problem, Colonel. Now, if I accidentally violated one of your orders, I apologize. But I just couldn't see any reason to take a shelling and not fight back."

Travis drew closer, trying to get out of earshot of the men who were standing there watching and listening. Finally he gave up and said simply, "Let's go to my headquarters."

As soon as they entered the tiny room, Travis spun around. "All right, I'll accept your apology about that incident just now. You know your own supplies and if you feel you have enough, that's fine.

"But, I've just been informed that you have three women with you and that they plan on fighting."

Here it comes, thought Brown. "That's correct."

"Well, I won't have that. The women must be moved to the chapel for their own protection."

Brown pulled one of the rough chairs away from the table, put a foot on the seat, and rested his elbow on his knee. He spoke gently. "Travis, you're making it hard for me to respect my decision of offering you help. The women in my command are every bit as competent as the men. They are versed in small unit tactics, thoroughly familiar with the care and use of small arms, including the two mortars we brought along, and they are experts in unarmed combat and karate."

"What's a karate?"

Brown smiled, "An ancient form of fighting developed by several oriental peoples."

Travis nodded and said, "Ah." He moved to the window and opened the shutters so that he could look out onto the courtyard. On the roof of the hospital, several men were working to repair a scaffolding. From beyond the walls came the continual boom of the Mexican batteries as they attempted to pound holes in the Alamo walls.

"Look, Brown," said Travis as he rubbed the back of his neck, "I don't want to tell you how to run your command, but since you entered the gate, you all have been under my command. While I welcome all the help I can get, I don't like the idea of women fighting. I know that my men won't like it, either. Besides, no matter what you say, the women are at a disadvantage."

"But they're not," countered Brown.

"We could argue this all day and never reach agreement. I'm afraid . . ."

"You're right, Travis," Brown cut in. "But there's a way to settle it. In fact, a couple of ways. Why not set, say, five targets and see who can knock them down faster from one-hundred yards? And, how about a wrestling contest between one of your men and one of my women?"

"That's out. No wrestling."

"Then between one of my men and one of the women," argued Brown. "That won't violate any of your prejudices but will show you what the women can do."

Travis turned away from the window. "I don't know about this. I don't like the idea of putting women on the same footing with men."

"All I can tell you is that two of our women have been in combat before and both have been awarded medals for heroism under fire."

"Set up the test. I'll watch, but I won't promise anything more."

SEVENTEEN

After breakfast, which consisted of supplies they had brought because Brown had been afraid of disease or dysentery incapacitating his people, Thompson decided that she wanted to personally meet some of the men of the Alamo. From the map that Millsaps had shown them earlier, she knew that Davy Crockett would be near the chapel, defending a log palisade that the Colonel considered the weakest point in his defense. After years of Davy Crockett lore, started by Walt Disney, Thompson found herself excited about seeing the real Davy Crockett. There were butterflies in her stomach.

She left the tiny room that she had shared with Meg Clark and Mary Jo Andross. Brown had thought long and hard about the separation and decided that while it might weaken his own case with Travis, it was equally true that men and women needed some privacy from each other. He had found the room and told them to take it.

As she walked along the buildings on the east wall, she

heard the first deep booms that signalled the beginning of the cannonade. Almost at the same time, she saw Brown and one of the Texans charge across the courtyard to the southwest corner of the fort. Instead of following them, she decided to head for the log palisade.

Crockett and his men were strung out along the wall, kneeling so that they were partially protected. Thompson knew which one was Crockett because he wore the coonskin cap that legend demanded. She was mildly surprised to see it, believing that it was something invented in Hollywood. She ran up and crouched beside Crockett and peeked over the logs. In the distance she could just barely see an old building with a dirt breastwork near it. As she watched, a cloud of smoke erupted from it, followed by a muffled boom and then a dull thud as a cannonball hit the wall near the south gate.

Crockett looked at Thompson and said, "They're terrible shots. Never hit anythin' important." He looked at her closely and was startled. "Hey, you're a female."

"I'm glad you noticed."

"Twarn't easy in that outfit."

Thompson looked down at her jungle fatigues and flack jacket. She could see where it would be hard to tell without a good look. And, since Crockett had shoulder-length hair (which was greying, she noticed), the length of her own hair didn't provide much of a clue, either. "You must be Davy Crockett."

"There are those who say I am."

"I've heard about you ever since I was a little girl. You're practically a legend. You and Jim Bowie."

"I don't know about me, but Jim Bowie sure is." Crockett was about to say more, but the sound of cannon fire reached them and they all ducked.

One of the cannonballs hit high chapel walls, bounced back, fell to the ground, and rolled into the stream.

Thompson watched as it rolled into the water. She looked at Crockett and asked, "Does this go on all the time?"

"Quite a bit of it. They haven't hurt anyone yet." Crockett patted the cannon beside him. "I told Colonel Travis we ought to fire back, but he won't waste the powder." He hesitated before continuing, "What's your name?"

"Jessica Thompson."

"You ride in with that bunch last night?"

"Sure did. If it hadn't been so late, I would have been looking for you sooner. You, and Jim Bowie, and Jim Bonham, and some of the others."

"Bonham's out tryin' to scare up some reinforcements. Going to bring Fannin in from Goliad. How come you're here?"

Thompson shrugged. "I wanted to help out." She felt the lie stick in her throat, especially after what she had said the night before. But she couldn't very well tell Crockett that she had been tricked into traveling 144 years back through time so that a multinational conglomerate could steal a bunch of Mexican oil wells that wouldn't even exist for another century and a half. When she heard the recoilless rifle open fire, she turned toward the sound but couldn't see anything because the buildings on the south wall were in the way. She said, "Well, some of my friends are shooting back."

She got up to leave to see what was happening. Crockett didn't budge, so she asked, "Don't you want to watch?"

"Can't leave my post. Colonel Travis gets mighty upset about that sort of thing. Besides, I wouldn't want to miss out on all the fun if they decide to attack us."

Thompson crossed from the courtyard but didn't venture up onto the parapet. She heard the cheering, knew that Brown had engineered some kind of success, and was about to go congratulate him when she saw Travis rush up.

They talked and then left, heading toward the west wall.
Thompson let them go.

An hour later Brown found her on the northwest wall,
looking at San Antonio. She was staring at the huge red
flag that flew from the church tower. Brown said simply,
"Jess, grab one of the M-14's and meet me in about five in
front of headquarters."

When she arrived, there were already several men there,
waiting. Brown introduced her to Travis and then told her,
"You'll be shooting against one of his men. It's that thing
we discussed last night."

Travis took over. "This is Bill Parks, one of our top
marksmen."

"Glad to meet you."

"Let's head up to the north wall. There's a good spot
there for this." Travis pointed the way. "There will be five
targets. Each man, or rather each person, will have only
one weapon. The first one to down all five targets will
win." Travis turned to Brown. "Acceptable?"

"Completely."

They cleared the men off the left side of the wall, and
one man set up a number of jugs and bottles and then
stepped off about one-hundred yards. With the edge of his
boot, he scraped a ragged line in the dirt.

"Behind the line," ordered Travis. "Are you both ready?
Good. When I give the word, the contest begins. And
now."

Almost simultaneously, Parks and Thompson squeezed
off the first shots. Parks' shot was a two-part process of
flint igniting first a powder train and then the tightly
packed powder in the breech. There was a great deal of
smoke. Thompson's weapon's flat "blam" was lost in the
noise of the flintlock but, while Parks was lowering his
weapon to reload, Thompson squeezed off an additional

four shots, shattering all her targets. She glanced at Travis, sighted again, and took out Parks' remaining four targets before he had time to get out his powder horn.

Travis stared at the M-14 and Thompson for a few seconds and then waved a hand. "I concede that your women can shoot. If your conscience is clear go ahead and use them." He turned and stomped back to headquarters, realizing as he went that it was the second time that morning that Brown had challenged his authority and won.

EIGHTEEN

Travis was sitting in his dingy headquarters room, trying to write a message to Sam Houston, but having little luck with it. He wanted to write something that would force Houston to send more men. Although John Sutherland insisted that Fannin was on his way, Travis didn't believe it. He had very little respect for Fannin. He would believe it when Fannin rode through the south gate, and not before.

He had just dipped the quill in the ink when someone knocked on the door. He shoved the quill into the pot, stacked his papers, and aligned the edges by bouncing the bottoms on the table. "Come on in."

Almeron Dickinson, the artillery officer, stepped through the door. "Sir, we'd like permission to fire the eighteen-pounder."

"What for?"

"Will Blazeby suggested that maybe we ought to let Santa Anna know that we got reinforcements, and he figured as how a shot from the eighteen-pounder ought to do it."

Travis rocked back in the flimsy wooden chair and laced his fingers behind his head. "You realize we have a critical shortage of powder?"

"Yes, sir, but I can't see where one shot, more or less, would hurt."

Travis rubbed his eyes hard with the heels of both hands. The strain was beginning to show but, more importantly, he was beginning to feel it. Just once, he wished he could forget everything, forget checking the supplies to make sure they didn't run out of powder, or meat, or lead balls. Just once, he wished he could forget about posting sentries and then checking to make sure they stayed at their posts. Just once, he wished someone else could take over the burden and do the worrying about it all. He glanced at Dickinson and could tell by the look in his eyes that Dickinson wanted very much to fire the cannon. Travis realized that this would be the best thing he could do. It would boost the morale.

"All right, Dick. Make the preparations. I'll be along in a couple of minutes."

As Travis walked up, he saw that almost everyone in the garrison was already there, anxious to watch. They had formed on the roof of the guardhouse, on the cannon emplacement, and on the artillery command post, all in the southwest corner of the fort. Travis stood on one side of the cannon; Brown was on the other, holding the cigar with which he would light the fuse.

Dickinson said proudly, "We aimed it at the large house close to the church there on the Military Plaza. We ain't sure, but we think it might be Santa Anna's headquarters, cause there always seems to be a lot going on there."

"Good choice," agreed Travis. He looked at Brown who had been given the honor of firing the shot, since he was the commander of the reinforcements. "You ready?"

"Sure."

But, before Brown could light the fuse, one of the artillerymen said, "Why not let one of the girls do it?"

"Brown?" said Travis.

Brown looked toward the ground. "Kimball. Find Jessie or Meg and get one of them up here."

From the back of the crowd, Jessie pushed her way forward. "I'll be happy to try to blow up Santa Anna's headquarters." She hoped that the defenders would interpret her remark as enthusiastic rather than indicative of prior knowledge, because she knew that the shot would hit the headquarters. Millsaps had briefed them on it.

Those thoughts stirred something else. Here she was, about to touch off a shot that had been fired in the original battle by someone else. Would her part make a change or would history worry, if indeed history could worry, about who lit the fuse? Dickinson and his men had loaded the cannon and aimed it.

It wasn't something that she could concern herself with at the moment. Brown laughed as he handed her the cigar, saying, "It's a real honor to turn this duty over to you, ma'am."

She mock bowed. "Thank you, Colonel."

"Anytime you're ready," said Travis.

Before she touched the fuse, Thompson took in the view. From that corner of the Alamo she could see a hairpin bend in the San Antonio River, the edge of the town that lined its bank, the Military Plaza that was bordered on one side by the San Fernando Church where Santa Anna had raised his red flag, and a large house, which Millsaps had said belonged to the Yturri family and that was being used as the headquarters.

She put the cigar to her lips and puffed on it until the end was glowing brightly. Around her the men cheered. She touched the fuse, saw it sputter and ignite and burn with a plume of blue smoke. The cannon jumped back with the recoil of the shot as smoke billowed from the barrel. The explosion was incredibly loud.

Moments later they saw part of the roof on the Yturri house jump and burst into pieces. She had scored a direct hit.

The men around her cheered again, slapping her on the back and shoulders. She didn't mind, too much, because she had suddenly been accepted as one of the defenders. Travis hugged her and said, "One hell of a shot. One hell of a shot."

"That probably stirred old Santy Anny up, don't you think, Colonel," said Dickinson.

"If it didn't, it should have." Travis looked at the men. "Gentlemen, and ladies . . ." He was interrupted, as he said it, by wild cheering. He started again, bowing to the crowd. "LADIES and gentlemen, I hate to sound like the commander, but since I am, I will ask you to return to your posts. Failing to convince you of the need for that, I ask that we disperse, so that the Mexicans can't get even with one shot."

The defenders even cheered that. They felt omnipotent. Thirty-three brave men and women had ridden to their aid, and it seemed that Fannin was coming as well. They could see the logic in spreading out and followed the order, slowly filtering into the courtyard and then breaking into small groups as they headed in the direction of their posts.

NINETEEN

Long before dark, Brown and his second-in-command, Jim McGee, strolled around the Alamo, checking defenses, comparing the actual fort with the maps that Millsaps had provided, and looking for clues that would confirm the accuracy of the Corporate information. They started at the headquarters, walked up the cannon ramp, and stepped onto the roof of one of the buildings that lined the west wall. They stepped over the 18-inch-high wall that bordered the roof. Glancing due west, they could see open ground for about 500 yards and then the San Antonio River. Across the river was the town, but there wasn't any activity. Brown thought that was strange since they couldn't see any cooking fires, and the Mexicans would have to go somewhere to eat.

They moved to the south, walking across the wooden parapet that had been erected by Green Jameson and the Texas engineers. It covered the breaks between buildings so that there was a continuous walkway along the west wall. At the Artillery Command Post, they stopped and Brown said, "Even if Millsaps is wrong, I doubt that there will be much of an attack from this end. Too much open ground."

McGee pointed to the river that approached the corner of the fort. "Seems like there is good cover from the south-west."

"Right. From the southwest."

While Brown held the top of a rickety ladder that con-sisted of crosspieces lashed to two poles with rope, McGee climbed down. When they were both on the ground, Brown said, "No need to inspect the cannon emplacement. I looked it over carefully while Jessie was blowing up buildings."

They climbed to the top of the guardhouse which was on the south wall. Its roof was about five feet below the top of the wall. To get to the rest of the emplacements, they had to climb up another three feet. The first building was actually the roof that covered the gate. Brown leaned over the wall and looked at the cannon emplacements set just outside the fort.

"We're going to lose those in the first few minutes of the assault."

McGee merely nodded.

They moved toward the end of the wall and Brown knelt on one knee, surveying the area carefully. To his left was the log palisade that Davy Crockett defended. In front of him was the road to Gonzales and across it was the house that had hidden the battery that Brown and his men had blown up earlier in the day with the recoilless rifles.

As they climbed down from the roof, Brown said, "I can see why we'll have problems here. I wonder if we can convince Travis to burn some of those houses to increase the killing zone."

They stopped at the chapel, went inside, and then up to

the remains of the roof where there were two cannons. The view to the south and east was unobstructed. Brown pointed to the low hills and said, "They have good cover for staging areas, but that's one hell of a run under fire."

They left the chapel and checked the corrals by using the doors cut in the wall. Both pens were surrounded by high walls and there was one cannon emplacement. McGee said, "It's too bad we can't let them come over that wall and corner them in here."

"I doubt they would be dumb enough to fall into a trap like that."

"They might, if they thought everyone was busy fighting on the other walls."

Although they knew practically nothing about medicine, other than combat first aid, they inspected the hospital. It was on the second floor of the tall barracks that lined the east wall. Cots had been set up, and there were some primitive bandages stored in a high wooden cabinet, but there was no one there.

"Either their medicine is extremely good, or they don't know enough to worry about manning the hospital," said McGee. "I better have Bob Cochran and Sam Holloway see what they can do with this place.

"Which reminds me. We should stop in to see Jim Bowie. He's in a room somewhere on the south wall."

On the north wall, they stopped to study the assault approaches. Brown didn't see any good way to get to the fort because of all the open ground. He knew that there would be an attack there and that it would reach the Alamo, but he couldn't see how to do it without losing a lot of men.

Having completed the survey, Brown said, "Looks like Millsaps and his researchers did a good job on this. It all checks, with the exception of a few minor details, but I guess that's to be expected."

McGee rubbed the back of his neck, surprised to find that he was sweating, even though the temperature wasn't very high. "So, now what?"

"We wait and see how things develop."

McGee ducked reflexively as a cannonball hit the wall.

Brown laughed and said, "Get used to it. They're going to keep it up for the rest of the siege. By the way, Millsaps claims that no one will be injured by it and in fact, there will be no casualties until the final assault begins."

"It's nice to know all this so that we don't have to worry."

Brown looked at his watch and then glanced around the Alamo self-consciously. Watches, at least wrist watches, hadn't been invented or weren't extensively used in 1836. Brown didn't know which and didn't really care. He just didn't want to add to all the other rumors about the strange people who came to help and the strange things they brought with them. He said to McGee, "I'll see you at dinner."

TWENTY

After Brown made the guard duty assignments that Travis had requested, he and Jessie went for a walk. Torches had been fastened to the interior walls and there were a few fires, but they only made flickering splotches of light that did little to chase away the gloom.

"They're really primitive here, aren't they?" said Brown quietly.

"What did you expect?"

Brown stopped and looked at the south wall. Spanish guitar music drifted over it. "That I couldn't answer. I suppose something like we had in Vietnam. The country didn't, or couldn't, supply some of the civilization that we were used to, so MACV took care of it. We had electricity, radio, television, and lights." He waved a hand around the walls. "They don't have any of that here."

"Did you notice how things quieted down at dusk?"

"Sure."

Jessie started walking again.

"That's because they're used to having very little light after dark. It kind of explains the tradition of moving at first light, or starting work in the early morning when it would probably be more efficient for a company to start business later in the day."

They walked through the gate in the short stone wall that separated the main plaza from the chapel courtyard. Crockett and his men were still there, crowded around a tiny fire and talking among themselves. Brown could just make out the shape of the guard, standing on the parapet of the buildings on the south wall.

At the massive wooden door to the chapel, they stopped. Brown examined the hinges, surprised that they were metal, and then wondered at his surprise. The people of that period had had metal for centuries. Brown pushed and the door swung open silently. The inside was wrapped in gloom. The lack of a roof over part of the building let in just enough light from the quarter moon to chase the shadows.

Brown hitchhiked a thumb over his left shoulder. "The powder magazine is in there. It's probably the best protected part of the fort."

Thompson pulled a tiny flashlight out of her pocket and switched it on. She swept the faint beam around the interior, revealing a slate floor and several small rooms. She said, "I'm surprised that it's so clean. Relatively speaking."

"Yeah, me too." He pointed to one of the rooms. "I think these were used by the monks." He noticed that one doorway had bars across it rather than a wooden door.

Thompson moved forward, and stepped into one of the cubicles. "Hey, have you been in here?"

"No. McGee and I were in the chapel and up on the cannon emplacement, but that's all."

"Well, take a look." She stepped back, pointing the light

into the room. It was fairly clean although there was a dirty remnant of a woven rug on the floor. The window had been bricked up, but that was apparently the only change made in the place after the Franciscans abandoned it in 1795. There was a desk with long wooden legs and a broken drawer sitting against one wall and a bed near the other. Thompson walked over to it and hit it once in the center. A cloud of dust set her to coughing.

"Damn. I should have brought a blanket."

Brown nodded. "That explains a lot. You took quite a chance on there being something available in here."

She laughed. "No. I checked it out before. Not close enough, I guess."

"What's wrong with that room I assigned to you and Meg and Andross?"

"You just said it. It's for me and Meg and Mary Jo. I can't kick the others out so that I can . . . well, never mind."

With her knee she shoved the bed to the wall and then sat down with her back against the wall. When she snapped off the light, she didn't like the way everything vanished and turned it back on. She leaned over to set it on the lip of the sill where there had once been a window.

Brown closed the door and saw an old wooden bolt on it. He slid it home and moved to the bed, unbuckling his pistol belt. He set it on the floor near the bed and reached over to unbuckle Thompson's. "This is the first time I've ever had to do this for a woman."

"You do it quite well."

He set her pistol beside his. "Thank you." He unbuttoned the top of her jungle fatigues and reached inside.

"Who the hell told you to wear a T-shirt?"

She shrugged her shoulders so that the fatigue jacket fell away, revealing the olive drab cotton undershirt. In the dim light, Brown could see that her nipples were erect. She wasn't wearing a bra. She allowed his hand to roam her chest as she shifted slightly to get closer so that she could unbutton his shirt.

Brown's hand drifted to her belt, which he unbuckled, and then began to unbutton the pants. "If you have on GI shorts, I think I'll go back and talk to Travis."

She lifted her hips so that he could slide the fatigue pants over them. When he saw the tiny, cream colored, lace panties, he said, "Hey. I like these. You can see right through them."

"Not exactly standard issue, but I had to have something to make me feel like a woman."

Brown let his hand rub the inside of her smooth, warm thigh. "I think you feel like a woman. Maybe even better than most."

"Maybe?"

"Definitely."

Brown reached down, untied her boots, and slipped them off her feet. He then pulled her fatigues the rest of the way off so that she was wearing only the undershirt, panties that hid nothing, and knee-high, green, army-issue socks. Brown didn't move for a moment. He just looked.

Thompson twisted and leaned back, resting on her elbows, looking at him. She moved her hips to excite him more.

Instead, he sat down on the edge of the bed and methodically began removing his boots, taking his time while she rubbed herself against him. When he finished, he rolled to one side, lifted his feet and gathered her into his arms. Brown slipped his hand between their bodies, first lifting her shirt and pushing down her panties.

It was after midnight when Brown awoke with a start. He looked up and in the fading light of the flashlight, he could see Thompson across the room. She had put on her socks, panties, and fatigue jacket. It covered her as well as some of the short skirts the girls had worn in the late 1960s. She was standing with her back to him, rummaging through the old desk.

Brown rolled to his stomach, set his chin on his hands, and said, "Anything happening?"

"No. Some interesting things in here, though."

"I like your modification of the fatigue uniform. Should be standard issue for all women." Brown wasn't interested in discussing anything that she might find in the desk.

She closed the desk and turned. "It could be very unhandy for the women. We couldn't bend over, crouch down, run or sit because everything would hang out."

"Can't see that as a disadvantage."

She stepped to him and waited until he looked up so that she could kiss him lightly on the lips. "Hadn't we better reappear?"

"Not really. Millsaps briefed me carefully on the next few days. The only thing that's supposed to happen is Travis sending out another messenger, but that won't be until tomorrow night. He'll change his mind, if he hasn't already."

"Won't everyone wonder about us?"

"So who cares? McGee can cover anything that will happen. Besides, I wouldn't be surprised if everyone knows where we are and what we're doing."

"I suppose not."

Brown wasn't sure how she was reacting since he couldn't see her face well in the dim light. He thought that she might be embarrassed by his practicality and attempted to soften it by asking, "Who's with Meg?"

Thompson hesitated and then said simply, "Pete Bailey."

"And Andross?"

"I suppose, when she left, it was to find her friends,

Kent and Cunningham. The three of them stick pretty close to each other."

"Ah." Brown sat up and reached for his clothes to begin dressing.

Thompson made a move toward hers but Brown stopped her by saying that he wanted to look at her for a few more minutes. Although Brown had said nothing to those in his command, he was worried about the Mexicans. He knew that the army outside the walls was growing larger every hour and, while he believed there was no way they could take the fort, he knew that some of his people were going to die, body armor or not. He was afraid, not for himself, but for Jessica. He wanted to protect her, give her some assignment that would keep her out of the battle, but he knew that he couldn't. The men would see it for what it was, and that would undermine his authority. In no way could he show favoritism. His involvement with her, however accidental or incidental, had to be carefully regulated for the sake of unit morale. Fortunately, Thompson understood that. Besides, he knew she wouldn't allow him to accord her any special treatment. Too chauvinistic.

Almost as if she had read part of his thoughts, she said, "Have you thought about what I said last night?"

"Yes, Jessie, I've thought about it. Almost continually. I have a few things that I want to discuss with all of our people before any decisions are made."

"What are you planning to do?"

Brown finished buttoning his shirt and reached for her hand. He pulled her to him and made her sit down. He let their hands fall to her thigh so that he could feel the taut, warm skin. He took a deep breath. "I'm going to tell them that we can't let H. Perot Lewis win. We can win the battle, but we can't return to our own time."

Thompson jerked almost as if she had been shot. "What do you mean, saying we can't return?"

Brown squeezed her hand as his mind raced. "It's all confused right now. I've been trying to sort it out, and it sounds like this. I took a job to defend a small outpost from government troops, supposedly to topple an African government. The situation here is basically the same. I signed documents saying I would perform this task."

She pulled her hand away from his. "But those documents mean nothing. They were signed under false pretenses."

"There's no question that legally you're right. Ethically, you're probably right, too, so there is no reason for me to feel any loyalty to the Texas-American Oil Company."

"But?" she said, knowing there had to be one.

"But—just what we said last night. I can't abandon the men here. That's it."

"Shit."

"Maybe. But that's the way I feel."

"You have no right to make that decision for the rest of us."

Brown recognized hysteria creeping into her voice and didn't understand it. He knew of her record in Vietnam and had seen the psychological profile that had been made of her. She was a person who wouldn't crack under any strain. He said, gently, "I have every right."

She sat in silence as the batteries in her flashlight continued to grow dimmer. She sobbed once and then sniffed.

"Jessie, what's wrong?"

She turned her head and mumbled, "Nothing."

"Just so you know I don't want Lewis to pull this off, either. We'll do something to prevent it. We'll all discuss it sometime tomorrow."

Without a word, she reached down, picked up her pants, and stood so that she could put them on.

As she buckled her belt, Brown picked up her gun and

held it out. "We'll think of something, I don't even have all of this time-travel nonsense worked out."

"Let's go," she said.

He reached for her, but she pulled away. Brown said, "Jessie. Don't be . . ."

She slid the bolt on the door. Brown grabbed her flashlight and followed her out of the chapel.

TWENTY-ONE

The morning of March third brought little relief from the bombardment. Brown had been awake for almost an hour when he heard a tremendous crash followed by a shattering impact on the north wall. He leaped up, shook his head at his questioning men and bolted outside. Travis was running toward the wall and Brown angled to catch him.

On the cannon emplacement, they crouched so that they could see over the wall without exposing themselves to Mexican rifle fire. To the northeast, not more than 250 yards away, two heavy cannons were surrounded by a protective breastwork that had been built in the dark. As they watched, there were twin plumes of smoke, twin crashes, and two cannonballs that hit the western end of the north wall, shattering the adobe and causing it to cascade to the ground.

"The walls were never meant to take this kind of punishment," said Travis.

"Can your sharpshooters do anything about it?"

Even as Brown asked the question, two men opened fire, but the Mexicans were being careful. There were momentary targets, but before a man could aim, the target was gone. The defenders were succeeding only in ensuring that the Mexicans kept their heads down, and were using the dangerously low reserves of powder.

"How about your people?"

Brown shrugged. "We can take out those cannons easily enough with either a recoilless rifle or a mortar."

Both men ducked, as another volley was fired, hitting the north wall in the same place. Adobe showered off the inside of the wall.

"If they keep that up long enough, they'll breach the wall."

Brown agreed, "They're really pumping the rounds through those things, aren't they?"

As another volley was fired, Brown, still crouching low, ran down the cannon ramp, straightening as he reached the bottom. He saw Dennison dodging across the central courtyard and called, "Get one of the recoilless rifles and get up here."

Dennison nodded and diverted toward the storage area. Brown ran for the barracks. He burst in, saw three of the men and Meg working on equipment that had gotten wet when the drizzle began at sunup. A cold north wind hadn't helped, coating some of the metal surfaces with slush.

"A couple of you grab some rifles and head up to the north wall."

Meg picked up one of the M-14's and found her field jacket. "I didn't know it could get so cold so fast."

They heard two more cannonballs strike the wall and felt the vibrations through their feet. Brown said, "Hurry up. We've got to move."

The others dropped their oil cloths and picked up weapons. Brown ran back outside and turned for the cannon ramp on the north wall. A dozen Texans were already there, trying to stop the Mexicans, but with no success. As Brown reached the ramp, Travis touched off a volley from his two cannons and the Mexicans responded. Theirs was the better shot. It took a hunk nearly six feet wide out of the top of the wall.

Almost immediately there was the dull bam of the recoilless rifle. Brown saw Clarke and the others scrambling up one of the ladders to take firing positions. Travis stepped away from his cannon to watch.

Two more Mexican shots hit the wall, and huge chunks were blasted loose. The breach was eight feet wide now and extended to within four feet of the ground. Dennison was firing the recoilless rifle as fast as he could reload it. Waters had joined the others and was about to fire an Ingram. Brown shouted at Waters to stop him. He didn't want to use the fully automatic weapons unless absolutely necessary.

The firing increased in intensity. More Texans joined the battle, taking potshots at the Mexican breastwork. Dennison finally dropped a round right where he wanted it. One of the Mexican cannons was destroyed, the other knocked off its base.

There was a cheer as Dennison became the hero for the second time in two days. He was shaking hands when a volley of Mexican rifle fire slammed into the fort.

One round cleared the wall and hit Micajah Autrey in the head. He dropped his rifle, reached up as he staggered backward, and then toppled over the log wall set to protect the cannon. While Clarke and the mercenaries kept the Mexicans busy, several of the Texans rushed to Autrey.

Thompson was the first to reach him. She pushed the collar of his jacket to the side and felt for his pulse but found none. Looking up, she saw Brown staring. She shook her head.

Several Texans picked up Autrey's body and carried it toward the hospital. On the parapets, the fight continued, with Texans and mercenaries trading ineffective fire with the Mexicans. Travis ordered the Texans to shoot only when they had a good target and left for the headquarters.

Gradually, over the next hour, the firing tapered off until it ended. Brown stayed to watch the whole time, aware of Thompson near him, ignoring him. He was also aware that something else, something in the back of his mind, was bothering him, nagging at him, but he didn't know what it was. He replayed the incidents of the last hour in his mind, knew that it was in there somewhere, but couldn't find it. Finally he gave up, figuring that he couldn't force it to the front. He would have to leave it alone until it popped up voluntarily.

TWENTY-TWO

When the shooting ended, Thompson left her post on the
north wall, drifting throughout the central courtyard, studying the Alamo. More than anything, she was amazed by its
size. She had always associated just the chapel with the
Alamo, not knowing that it was really only a small part of
the entire mission.

As she reached the south wall, the steady drizzle that
had been depressing them all day began to let up. To the
west were patches of blue sky and a promise of sun to
warm the afternoon. That, and their earlier victory with the
Mexican cannons buoyed her spirits. She climbed to the
parapets on the south wall.

Thompson was looking to the southeast when she saw a
troop of Mexican cavalry appear, gallop over one of the
low hills, and angle off toward a ravine that paralleled part
of the road from Gonzales. She couldn't see the reason for
their hurry, only that they were whipping and spurring their
horses, trying for more speed.

Thompson slipped the sling of her M-14 and jacked a round into the chamber, not sure what was happening. The Mexicans suddenly wheeled and charged directly toward the fort. They were just over 800 yards away.

A lone horseman popped into view about 100 yards in front of the Mexicans. He broke to the left, away from the south wall, briefly, and then turned back toward it. Several clouds of smoke erupted from the Mexicans as they ineffectually fired their pistols from an extreme range. That told Thompson all she needed to know: the lead horseman was a Texas courier.

To her left she saw several of Davy Crockett's Tennesseans scramble to turn their cannon so they could fire on the Mexicans. The shot was wide and they hurried to try again.

Even though they were still over 500 yards away, a dozen Texans began firing, apparently hoping to slow the pursuit. Thompson thumbed the adjustable sights of her M-14 and began to shoot.

The gap between the courier and the Mexicans was closing faster than the distance between the rider and the fort. Thompson squeezed off the rounds almost as fast as she could pull the trigger.

From the roof of the chapel came another cannon shot. It missed, but several of the cavalrymen pulled up and turned, riding away from the fort. A half-dozen others ignored the shooting, trying to stop the Texan before he reached safety.

Momentarily, it looked good for the Texan. But another group of riders, coming from LaVillita, joined the chase. They were between the fort and the rider, but they weren't outside the range of the Texan guns in the Alamo. Nearly all the riflemen switched to the new targets. Two of the group fell from their saddles. The others continued, the banners on their pikes flapping and their armour flashing as the sun broke through for the first time.

When the courier spotted the new threat, he turned north but there were Mexican infantrymen there, blocking his escape. Several of them fired, but the range was far too great.

The rider turned once more, this time heading straight for the palisade guarded by Crockett. The Tennesseans there, as well as the Texans on the south wall, opened fire with everything they had, trying to protect the courier. Thompson saw another Mexican fall and then two more.

The group from La Villita looped farther to the south, trying to ride out of the range of the Texans but still cut off the rider. That was enough. The loop took them too far in the wrong direction and by the time they had turned north again, the rider was past them.

When the courier was less than 100 yards from the Alamo, and the Mexicans more than 300, they reined to a halt, dived off their horses and opened fire in a last-ditch effort to kill the courier. The rider hugged the neck of his horse, showing as small a target as possible.

Reaching the stream near the south wall, the horse leaped across, took two steps, and tried to clear the palisade, but stumbled just inside the fort, throwing the rider, who rolled several times but came up grinning.

With the courier safely inside the Alamo, there was nothing more for the Mexican cavalry to do but mount their horses and hastily ride out of artillery range.

The courier stood shakily, held up by two of Crockett's men. Travis ran up and grabbed the man's hand. He said, "I'm not going to welcome you back, but I'm sure as hell glad you're here."

"You won't be when I tell you the news."

Travis looked at the gathering crowd. "Let's go to my

headquarters and then you can tell me about your mission."

"Let me check my horse first."

The animal wasn't injured and was led away to the corral. Together, Travis and the courier walked away. Thompson asked one of the men standing next to her who the courier was.

"That's Jim Bonham. He was supposed to bring Fannin from Goliad."

"Do you think he succeeded?"

The man turned toward the south, looking at the empty ground between the fort and the horizon. "Don't seem likely."

TWENTY-THREE

Travis called a meeting of the officers thirty minutes later, relaying Bonham's news that Fannin wasn't going to leave Goliad. He had hoped that they could pry Fannin out before it was too late, but he wasn't going to count on it any more. There was little time, even if they could persuade him to come. The other thing that disturbed Travis more than that was word that there were virtually no adult males in Gonzales. Although it was a small town, it seemed that nearly everyone had abandoned it to join Houston. It meant that they could count on help from no one.

It was decided that John W. Smith, one of the men who had ridden out on the afternoon the siege began to see if the Mexican army was close, would leave around midnight, and ride to Goliad to try to get Fannin to move. Failing that, he would ride on to Washington-on-the-Brazos, where the new Texas government was meeting, to try to enlist aid.

To cover Smith's departure, a small group would be sent

toward the sugar mill to stir up the Mexicans. They would try to blow up the battery, but it wasn't an imperative mission simply because the battery was so far from the fort and the cannons were so small. They had been there for nearly eleven days and had done very little damage to the fort.

Discussion about who would lead the diversionary party took the most time. Brown suggested that some of his men do it, since they were trained in counter-insurgency and covert operations. After explaining what counter-insurgency and covert operations meant, it was agreed that Brown's men should go.

Travis, in one of his moods, and remembering the lost contest and argument with Brown about the women, said, "I think that your expert rifleman, Thompson, should lead the raid."

Brown stood to protest, but Travis waved him down and continued. "You were the one who said that they could do anything any of the men could do."

"Yes, of course, but I . . ."

"Is she or isn't she capable of leading the raid?"

"Certainly. There's no doubt of that. But . . ."

"Fine. Then that's settled. After all, you said that she was an expert in small unit tactics."

Brown spoke slowly. "That I did." He realized that there wasn't much he could do. He had no doubt that Thompson could lead the men in the raid. In fact, he knew that any one of the people he had brought would be capable of it. It was just that he didn't like being maneuvered. But, then, Travis probably didn't like it, either, and he had certainly maneuvered Travis during the last few days. Besides, there was Millsaps' guarantee that no one had been seriously hurt during the first twelve days of the siege, so Thompson should have no problems.

And suddenly it was all out in front of him. Millsaps

talking about the incredible luck of Travis and the Texans during the first twelve days and then seeing Autrey fall off the cannon emplacement. Time had compensated and unplanned, or unknown, changes were taking place. Just because Millsaps had said something did happen was no longer a guarantee that it would.

Of course, major things seemed to remain the same. The Alamo was just as the maps described it. The breach was right where Millsaps said it would be. Bonham had ridden in just as it was outlined in the material that Millsaps carried. It could be that only minor items changed. If one could call the death of a fellow defender minor.

Brown realized that the others were staring at him. He ran a hand through his hair and said, "Thompson will lead. I'll send ten others. A full squad. What do you all have in mind?"

Travis asked that Thompson join them. When she arrived, they went over the plan carefully, coordinated the times, looked at maps, and then broke for dinner. There was nothing to be done, except to have a general briefing for Thompson's squad, until Smith was ready to leave.

At ten minutes after midnight on March 4, John W. Smith sat on a skittish horse under the arch of the south gate, waiting for the firing that would signal the beginning of the diversionary attack on the sugar mill. He pulled on the reins and patted the neck of the horse, trying to settle it, but there were too many people standing around.

Travis took hold of one rein. "You ready?"

"Yes, sir."

"Got everything?"

Smith touched the saddlebags. "In there. Got a couple of personal messages from some of the boys. Didn't think you'd mind."

"No. Of course not."

Travis checked his watch and then slipped it back into his pocket. "Any minute now." He looked over his shoulder. "Open the gate."

North of the fort, Thompson and the ten mercenaries crouched in the tall weeds that lined the marshy area near the northeast side of the San Antonio River. Thompson was using special night glasses to count the number of Mexicans working close to the three cannons. Near them she could see the old mill, a decrepit, decaying wooden and stone building. Behind a door that was hanging on one hinge, Thompson thought she saw movement. She tapped John Blair on the shoulder and he leaned close.

"You and two others watch the mill. There are some in there too."

"Right." He touched two shoulders, and the three of them quietly worked their way out of the marsh to a position where they could see two doors of the mill and several of the windows.

Without a word, Thompson moved forward, the rest of the squad stringing out behind her. One man with an Ingram stayed where he was to cover them, if necessary, during the retreat.

When they were in position, Thompson checked the time, shielding the ruby numbers of her digital watch so that no one but she could see them. Directly in front of her were the three cannons with three Mexican crews preparing to begin the bombardment again.

Thompson took a white phosphorous grenade from the huge pocket on the side of her fatigue jacket and pulled the pin with her left index finger holding the safety lever with her right hand. With her left, she signalled the others and when she dropped her hand, they all threw their grenades at the cannons. As she flattened herself, she heard the seven grenades explode.

Immediately she looked up but saw no movement. From

the men stationed around the doors to the sugar mill, she heard a volley of shots and saw two Mexicans fall as others dived back inside. Blair and his men were keeping them pinned down by pouring rifle fire into the old building. Apparently a bullet hit one of the Mexican powder supplies because there was a dull explosion followed quickly by three others and the building burst into flames.

As the flames built higher, Thompson saw Blair and his men, silhouetted against the fire, drop back toward the river. All resistance by the Mexicans ceased.

Thompson waved at the men with her and they began to creep backward, watching the horizon, waiting for the enemy assistance they were sure would be coming to help defend the cannons.

They reached the edge of the water and slipped into it, wading across the San Antonio in two relays, one covering the other. Thompson was sure that the Mexicans must have seen the brief firefight. She couldn't believe that no one had been sent to the rescue.

Once across the river, they began the run that would take them to the walls of the Alamo. They were strung out, several meters between them, with a flanker on each side separated from the main group by twenty meters. It made no difference. There was no pursuit.

The Mexicans, shocked out of their momentary stupor by the blazing sugar mill, rushed toward it. Cavalry patrols that normally roamed the hills around the Alamo, with nothing to chase except jackrabbits and Jim Bonham, galloped toward the flames. Several infantry patrols diverted toward the area, but not even one unit was fast enough to catch Thompson and her men. They were across the river and half-way back to the fort before the first Mexicans reached the burning mill.

Inside the Alamo, when they heard the first explosions, Smith moved through the gate to the fenced area outside the wall. A half-dozen men went with him. The six of them scattered toward La Villita both to flatten the shacks that obstructed the view from the fort and to create another diversion, giving Smith an even better chance to escape.

Smith didn't try anything fancy, but spurred his horse down the road, neither wavering nor slowing until he was far from San Antonio.

About thirty minutes after Smith left, and after Thompson and her squad had returned, Brown decided that everything had settled down enough for him to add his final touch to the battle. The claymore mines had been sitting, waiting for someone to place them and, after surveying the Alamo, Brown knew exactly where he wanted to put them. Without telling Travis, Brown asked the sentry to open the south gate so that he and ten of the mercenaries could go out to plant the mines.

Under Brown's direction, they began stringing the wire and placing the mines along the foot of the wall. Brown had thought that it would be the best position, because he could trigger them just as the Mexicans reached the wall, taking out the first two or three ranks as they tried to use their scaling ladders.

But, once outside, he noticed that the south bank of the stream was slightly higher than the north bank. It meant that something placed just under the top of the bank would have a clear field of fire back toward the wall. Brown grinned as he surveyed the scene. The mines, if placed facing the fort, would be unseen by the Mexicans. They would leap the stream in their haste to get to the wall. The claymores would be at their backs. The walls would protect the Texans. If Brown triggered the mines just as the enemy reached the wall, the shot would catch them from behind and might create enough confusion to break the assault right then.

In the dark, he had a hard time identifying Jim McGee, but once he found him, Brown whispered, "I've got an idea for a good gag. We'll put the claymores on the south side of the stream, facing the fort."

McGee stood silently for a moment and then said, "Are you out of your..." He stopped and looked at the bank, toward the fort, and back at the stream. He began to laugh. "Of course. That's perfect."

"We'll have to be careful not to give them too much elevation, though."

McGee nodded. "And we'll have to string two or three trip wires so that we can fire the things."

"Double up on all the firing mechanisms, to be on the safe side. If we bury the wires three or four inches under ground, the Mexicans won't see them."

"All right, Colonel." McGee turned away and ordered, almost in a normal tone of voice, "Stop digging. We're moving the mines."

TWENTY-FOUR

The battle didn't change on March 4. The Mexicans added cannons to the batteries that were pounding the fort, but the damage they caused was still minor. Far outside the walls, Mexican infantry continued to maneuver, always trying to find the gap that would complete the ring, keeping reinforcements out of the Alamo and the couriers in it.

Neither Brown nor Travis paid any attention to the Mexican troop movements. Travis, because he couldn't do anything about them, and Brown, because he already knew what they were doing. Periodically, one of the Alamo's cannons would fire on a Mexican unit, but more often, they just let the maneuvering continue unmolested. At 6:00 in the morning and again at noon, Travis had fired the 18-pounder, indicating that he still held the fort. He had told Smith before the courier rode out that he would fire it morning, noon, and night while the Texans were fighting. If there was no signal, it meant the Alamo had fallen.

In the early afternoon, when the sun's rays could be best

used to light the rooms on the east wall, Brown called a meeting of all the mercenaries. He had walked around the Alamo telling them that he wanted to talk to them at 2:30. Most were already there when he entered the room that they had been using as a barracks. It was twelve feet deep and twenty long. There were four windows in it and all of them were open. Brown had one of the men light several lamps so that the remaining gloom was chased away. He pushed one of the tables toward the center of the room. Behind it was a map of the Alamo that Millsaps had brought.

Near each window, Brown stationed his own men to keep the Texan defenders away. He had told Travis that it was important that he meet privately with his people, and Travis said that he would respect that privacy. Travis hoped that Brown wasn't intending to take his people out of the fort. Brown said that wasn't the purpose of the meeting.

Millsaps ran through a quick head-count and turned to Brown. "Everyone's here."

Brown sat on the table and let his feet dangle. He gripped the edge with both hands. "I guess the first thing to do is to define the purpose of this meeting. It seems superfluous to point out that Texas-American lied to us. But, we have the option of a number of choices and before we rush headlong into any action, we should take the time to analyze the situation."

Almost before Brown had finished speaking, Millsaps was on his feet. "You can't go deciding what you're going to do. You've already signed contracts." Millsaps waved a hand to indicate everyone. "You all have contracts."

"Bull SHIT." It was McGee.

"Let's not get emotional right now." Brown straightened and rubbed the bridge of his nose. "We've got some important things to discuss. I think Thompson should outline some of her thoughts before we go any further." Brown looked at Millsaps. "And I'll thank you to keep your damn mouth shut."

Thompson stood and leaned back against the dirty adobe wall, her mind spinning. She hadn't expected Brown to call this meeting and she hadn't expected him to make her state her case. She stared at the ceiling and tried to think. Finally she said, "This may be a bit disjointed, but the main points will be clear.

"The thing that I'm most concerned about is the power that we may be handing H. Perot Lewis by winning this fight. If we show him that he can make any change in history that he wants, suddenly he will control not only the destiny of the people who work for him, but all people who ever lived. Such power could only be abused."

From the back someone said, "So what?"

"So, I believe that we have a responsibility to keep Lewis from gaining that power by failing in our mission."

"Good GOD!" shouted someone.

"The only way to do that is to get killed," said someone else.

Brown stood. "You haven't thought this through. We could just leave. Late tonight. The Alamo would fall and Lewis would think that his plan failed."

McGee tried to break in. He had been selected not only for his combat experience, all in Vietnam, but because of his study of physics on the G.I. Bill after his discharge. Originally Brown couldn't understand why Travis and the corporation were so excited by his scientific background, but now he knew. McGee said, "I have been considering much the same thing for the last few days."

Thompson smiled, "And?"

"And, the way I see it, there are about three possibilities here. One is that no matter what we do, we're going to lose the battle because that is already history. Two, if we win, the world we go back to will be nothing like the one we left

because of our action here. The possibilities there are end-
less. For example, Lincoln will be assassinated in about
thirty years. What's to prevent someone from stopping
that?"

"And three, history will compensate in some way. From
the briefing that Millsaps gave us, I think some compensa-
tion is already taking place." There was a sudden eruption
of noise as a dozen people asked questions, but McGee
waved them to silence. "Again, an example. That man
Autrey being killed. According to history, no one is supposed to die until the final assault.

"If history compensates, then the world we go back to
will be only slightly altered. History books would record
the glorious Texas victory at the Alamo, maybe some land
changing hands, that sort of thing.

"Of course, all this is speculation. We have no way of
knowing because no one has ever done it before."

"But the important thing," broke in Thompson, "is to
make sure that H. Perot Lewis doesn't profit from our
being here."

Millsaps started to protest, but Brown silenced him with
an icy glance. Instead, Dennison said, "I would think the
important thing is to insure our survival. Without that, it
makes no difference who wins or loses."

Brown said, "There is one thing we don't know. What
was Lewis' reason for sending us back here? Maybe he just
decided that he didn't like the Texans losing?" He looked at
Millsaps and raised an eyebrow in question.

"I haven't the faintest idea. My whole job was to brief
you on the battle and see to it that you had the information
you needed to win."

"I don't think his reasons are important," said McGee.
"What we have to do is decide on some course of action."

Brown said, "I have to agree with Jessie on one point. I
don't think we should participate in anything that will give

Lewis any additional power."

"And," said McGee, "to answer your question. Anything that Lewis does is designed to gain additional power. That is the purpose behind this. What we don't know are the specifics."

"There should be some discussion here," said Brown. "I, for one, don't see us abandoning the men here. We have to see it through. Once that mission is complete, I think . . ." He hesitated. "I think that we should stay here. In this time. That way Lewis wouldn't know what happened to us."

McGee interrupted. "That also presents an interesting paradox. Would Lewis know that we have been sent? Would our changes here affect him in the future? In other words, any action we take is going to be unknown to him because it will affect him just as it does everyone else. If we don't go back to tell him the story, he won't know that he sent us."

"Jesus Christ," said Brown. "What did you just say?"

"I'm not really sure," laughed McGee. "But I think that I said that Lewis won't know if he won because he won't know that he sent us unless we go back and tell him he did."

"You can't seriously be thinking of staying here?" Millsaps sounded horrified.

"Why not?" It was Thompson. "Your company set up the requirements. No family. Most of us are here only because we could find nothing better in our time. Sure, we thought we were going overseas, but that makes little difference. We were all willing to risk death. Why not stay here and risk life? And, if what Jim says is right, it might not even be the same world. So why go back?"

For an hour they discussed staying in 1836 after they won the battle of the Alamo. The arguments remained the same. Defeat Lewis by not returning but remaining to help

the men in the Alamo. At first there were only a few of the
men who wanted to stay. Thompson argued persuasively
for staying. Brown did the same. They pointed out that
their knowledge, guarded carefully and used wisely, could
easily lead them to great fortunes. One man said that he
would change his name to Sutter and start a mill in Califor-
nia. There was laughter at the comment, but Brown
pointed out that it was basically what he had in mind. They
could be in Colorado for the Gold Rush there. They could
invest in railroads. Gas and electric companies. Making a
fortune wasn't that hard. And, they had the gold that Lewis
had provided in case they needed to buy anything before
they arrived at the Alamo, or if they had to bribe someone
to get them there. The gold, divided equally, would amount
to a little more than one-thousand dollars per man, or
woman, but it was a start. Besides, Brown was sure that
there would be benefits, land grants and so forth, for being
at the Alamo and taking part in the Texas War for Independence. All of it could be parlayed into a fortune by
people who were clever. The only thing they had to do was
use their money and their knowledge wisely, but Brown
said he wasn't worried about that. The people had all been
picked, not only for their combat skills but for their intelligence. They were the best and the brightest. Eventually,
there was only one dissenting vote. Millsaps. He had a
family in North Dallas, and he couldn't abandon them. He
had already realized that, morally, he couldn't go through
with Lewis' plan. But he didn't want to leave his family.
While they all sympathized with him, they wouldn't let
him go home. He had to stay. Thompson convinced him by
telling him that he could build a fortune and then arrange it
so that his wife and children would get it all. Lawyers and
banks could set up trusts. She didn't tell him that she
doubted his family would exist. She wasn't sure that it

wouldn't, but without him she didn't think so.

When the debate died, because everyone had decided to stay, Brown said, "One final point. We have the power to totally destroy Santa Anna's army, or at least the part of it that is here now. We could run the casualties unbelievably high, and cause questions to be asked. We want to maintain a low profile.

"To that end, I suggest that we don't use our weapons on full automatic, or trip the claymores, unless we are being overrun. We will do what we have to. We'll survive, but we don't want to make the Mexican defeat here too spectacular."

Dennison said, "Let me get this straight, Colonel. You want us to use single shot and not automatic."

"Right. Unless you're in a position where you need to use it to save your life. We want to win and survive."

"We may not have to worry about that," said Millsaps. "After the final assault, Santa Anna sent a communique to Mexico City saying that he had taken the Alamo with only seventy killed. He also claimed that there were over six hundred defenders.

"And ," he continued, "some sources claim that the defenders killed as many as four thousand Mexicans before the fort was lost. Our presence here shouldn't be of much consequence, in the historical accounts, with such wide discrepancies."

Brown finally said, "Then it's settled. We do our best to hold down the casualties, and we all leave after the final assault on March fifth. We'll leave as a body so we won't be recorded, historically, after that point. Once outside the fort, we can split up."

Brown checked his watch. "Anyone have any other questions? No. Then let's break up this meeting and get something to eat."

As they started to drift outside, Thompson stepped close to Brown and whispered, "I want to talk to you. How about the chapel again tonight? Late."

He looked up in time to see her smile. He nodded and then joined the crowd.

TWENTY-FIVE

While the mercenaries were meeting, Cunningham, Kent, and Andross were sitting on the parapet near the Alamo's headquarters. Cunningham and Kent had their backs to the wall and were watching Andross. She had taken off her boots and had rolled her pants almost to her knees. She was dangling her feet as if there was a pool to cool them in.

She said, "I'd like to know where these men came from."

"Which men?" Cunningham had unbuttoned the camouflaged shirt that Brown had given him so that the "University of Iowa, Idaho City, Ohio" legend was visible underneath.

"The ones we came with."

"Oh, don't be stupid, Mary Jo. They came from Texas-American. Who else would have known that we were all going to be gone? And who else could have arranged for someone to work the equipment?"

"And who was that?"

Kent cut in. "Williamson, of course. I thought he was spending all that time with us so that his name would be linked to the discovery, but he was learning what he needed to know to send the force back here."

Andross turned so that only one leg hung over the side. She pulled the other up and hugged it, resting her chin on her knee. "So what do we do?"

Kent sat up. "That's something that we really haven't considered."

"I would imagine," said Cunningham, "that we should help defend the place."

"Is that a good idea?" asked Mary Jo.

Kent looked at her carefully, knowing that there was more than just the surface of the question. He said, "How do you mean that?"

"We'll be changing history."

"We don't know that. Things may work themselves out. We have no way of knowing what will happen. All we can do is ride along, as we have been. We need to stay close to the mercenaries because they have the beacon."

Before either of them could respond to Cunningham, they saw Brown exit the building opposite them and look around the courtyard. He held a hand near his forehead to shield his eyes from the sun and squinted in their direction. He then waved once, almost as if he were telling the three of them to stay where they were. As he climbed the dirt ramp built so that the Texans could move cannons to the wall, Brown said, "Glad I found you people. I have some news."

"Go ahead and tell us," sighed Cunningham.

"I don't know exactly how to say this. I suppose that you should have been allowed in the meeting, but then, you are outsiders."

"Outsiders on everything," said Kent. "You and the

Texans and history. We don't belong anywhere."

Brown crouched, leaning a knee of the short wall that bordered the inside of the parapet. He picked up a handful of dirt and let it drain slowly through his fingers. Without looking up, he said, "We're going to stay in this time period."

Andross jerked upright, but neither Kent nor Cunningham moved. Cunningham said, "I suspected something like this."

"You did? Why?"

"That's not important. Why have you decided to stay?"

Brown ran through the explanation carefully, telling them why he couldn't let Lewis win. He knew, having met Lewis, that Lewis would twist time travel to his own purposes, had in fact already tried to, and yet, given the capability of stopping the Mexican army from overrunning the Alamo, Brown had to do that. The only way to accomplish both of these goals was to remain in 1836. He hoped that nobody would be greatly inconvenienced by it.

Kent said, "And our votes have no bearing on the decision?"

"It's been made," Brown said simply.

"You take a lot for granted. What's to stop us from getting together with Millsaps and escaping your tiny dictatorship?"

For the first time Brown looked up. "First, you're not in the same class with Millsaps. I think that more drives each of you than just self-interest. And if you consider the whole problem, you'll realize that it is in your self interest to stay here. To defeat Lewis."

Cunningham started to protest but Kent touched his sleeve and slightly shook his head. To Brown, he said, "You keep your beacon. We won't fight you on that point. Next time, though, ask us how we feel. It's the least you can do."

Brown stood up and glanced toward old San Antonio. Fires were already flickering in the shadows that grew as the sun dropped. "Next time I will. I just didn't think."

Cunningham waited until Brown was out of earshot. He turned on Kent and demanded, "What in the hell do you mean we won't fight him?"

Kent said, "If you think about it for a minute, you'll understand." He glanced at Andross and saw that she was smiling. "Mary Jo gets it."

And then Cunningham laughed. "Of course. We don't need the beacon. We can communicate with Tuck."

Kent nodded rapidly. "The only problem is finding a legal or banking firm who will follow our instructions and mail the damn letter in a hundred and fifty years."

"That shouldn't be too hard. Some of those eastern establishments pride themselves on going clear back to the Revolutionary War. And, they'll make sure the letter gets mailed, no matter how crazy they may think it is," said Mary Jo.

"That leaves the question of the location. Tuck gets the letter and it tells him we're here and need to be rescued. He sends someone back to locate us. How does that man find us?" Cunningham seemed puzzled.

"Easy," said Mary Jo. "We meet him at the Liberty Bell."

"Or here at the Alamo," said Kent. "Or even better, across from the lab. We ought to be able to get fairly close to it, even if all the landmarks we know will be missing."

"Not all of them," laughed Cunningham. "The hills and ravines won't change much. We'll be able to find the lab. This really is a scream. Tuck will probably laugh himself sick."

"We can leave the details until later. All we have to do is survive. And not let Brown know that we're going to return."

Andross said, "He might be right, you know."

"I'm sure he is," said Kent. "But Lewis will never know that we were here. All he knows is that he sent a force of mercenaries to the Alamo and they never came back. Tuck will get our letter, say the day after we disappeared, explaining where we are and everyone in Dallas thinks we were at Padre Island."

The light was now gone and around them defenders were lighting torches and cooking-fires. Cunningham stood up and started down the dirt ramp. "Let's get something to eat. Tomorrow is going to be very interesting," he said quietly. "Very interesting."

TWENTY-SIX

March fifth dawned warm and clear, a welcome relief from
the drizzle that had fallen most of the night. Nearly
everyone used the warm weather as an excuse to get outside. They came out of the chapel, the long barracks on the
east wall, from the headquarters where Travis still scribbled pleas for help that would never come, from the hospital, and the artillery barracks. They clustered in small
groups in the central plaza, tired men in dirty clothes who
knew that the end had to be near, and thirty-three strangers
in jungle fatigues who waited to change history.

Everyone in the fort seemed to sense a change in the
Mexican lines. Tents, campfires, and masses of men could
be seen all around the Alamo as the ring was completed.
There were still gaps, but even the most casual observer
could see that Santa Anna had nearly five-thousand soldiers surrounding the Texans. The final assault could be
only hours away. The Texans believed that; the mercenaries
knew it.

Late in the afternoon, the continual cannonade that had

pounded the fort steadily for the last two days suddenly
ceased. Brown realized what it meant and called his people
together for a final briefing in the northwest corner of the
chapel courtyard, sheltered by the one structure that would
survive not only the battle but the passage of time. Behind
him, along the short palisade built of pointed logs and dirt,
Davy Crockett and his Tennesseans waited patiently.

Brown sketched a rough map in the dirt as he said, "All
right, I know all of you have seen this before, but we're
going to study it one more time. Besides, I want to remain
a little flexible in case there are mistakes in all that jive
handed out by the corporation. And, we still don't know
what changes our influence in this time will have."

He drew a long arrow pointed straight at the palisade.
"As we all know, this is the weakest point in the fort,
followed closely by that breach in the north wall. The
Mexicans will strike straight for the palisade. I'll take half
of our people and wait there.

"Bromhead, since you're the best bayonet man, I want
you to form a flying squad with the other half to plug any
holes in the defenses. The whole attack will not come from
the south. Travis and his boys are going to need some help
shoring up the walls."

Brown nodded at the three new people. "Mary Jo, I
guess you can head for the hospital. We should stop the
assault long before it reaches you there. If not, I don't
think the Mexicans will harm you. According to history,
they killed the young sons of one of the defenders, but they
were careful not to harm the women.

"Andy, you and Cunningham might be the most useful
on the north wall. With our force concentrated in the south,
the north will be vulnerable. A couple of automatic
weapons up there might be just the thing. Any objections?"

"Just one," said Cunningham. "Why are you exiling us
to the north wall?"

"I'm not exiling you. We've all worked together for several weeks. We know each other and we know that the assault will be made or broken in the south. We can work together to stop it. But that doesn't mean things won't get tense in the north. We'll need someone there. You two seem to be the ideal choice."

"Okay, Colonel," said Kent. "We'll guard your backs."

Brown smiled, thinking that Kent's comment showed the kind of enthusiasm he had looked for when he had hired the rest of the force. He was lucky that fate had thrown him two men with some experience. He could just as easily have gotten people who had never seen a gun before.

He glanced around the rest of his group. They had been briefed, rebriefed, and then briefed again so that they knew everything that he had to say, but he asked for questions anyway. They had none. He looked at his watch and then toward the sun.

"About twenty minutes. I'm going to try to convince Travis that the attack is coming so that he doesn't screw around trying to decide that this is it. Remember, we want to be careful with our weapons." Without another word, Brown stood, rubbed his foot through the map, and turned toward headquarters. He could see Travis, obvious in the outlandish costume of red pants and homespun denim jacket, talking to three other men and pointing toward the north wall battery.

While his men and women took their places either at the south wall or in the flying squad, Brown crossed the dry creek and moved to Travis. He took a position just to the rear of the Texan commander and waited.

Travis glanced over his shoulder and then back to the men he had been talking to. "Jim, I want you to take over the battery on the chapel roof. That is, if you don't want to head back out to Goliad."

"Damn, Will, I'd never make it in time. You're going to need all the help you can get."

Travis nodded. "All right." He turned to John Baugh. "Listen, I want a meeting of all the officers in about thirty minutes in the headquarters. Spread the word. Make sure that Crockett gets it. I want him there."

"Colonel Travis? I think you should postpone that meeting for a while."

Travis scowled at Brown. "And I think you should let me run this command."

Brown shook his head. "I'm not contradicting you, only making a suggestion. I believe that the Mexicans are going to hit us in a few minutes."

Travis laughed. "You haven't been here long enough to make that judgment. They do this periodically to throw us off balance. They'll start the cannonade again about 10:00 tonight. I don't think Santa Anna will attack at dusk. That would give us cover to escape."

"He knows you won't try to escape. Besides, his reasoning is the same as yours. He wants to catch you with your pants down so that he can scramble over the wall to gain a foothold before you realize that this is a serious assault."

"Ah, Colonel Brown, we have been here for twelve days. We have observed the arrival of the Mexicans carefully, and we know that the majority of their army is somewhere between Bexar and the Rio Grande and probably won't arrive here for days yet."

"But there are nearly five-thousand troops out there now, and that kind of force should be able to take this fort."

"And a concentrated attack would do it, but Santa Anna will not attack in the evening."

There were two deep-throated bams that echoed through the fort. Travis glanced toward the south and said to Brown, "Your men firing?"

"Yes."

"I doubt that the Mexicans will be in range. We've had

quite a bit of luck making them keep their distance."

"Look, Travis, I'm not here to argue. The effective range of the scoped weapons we have is over a thousand yards. I've given my people permission to take out targets of opportunity. They were probably trying to hit the officers about to lead the assault."

Travis took a deep breath and started to walk to the south wall. "Why don't you show me this attack that you think is coming?"

They were only halfway there when the Mexican trumpeters began playing Deguello. "That tune means no quarter for the defenders," said Travis. "If they take the fort, they put the garrison to the sword."

"I know."

A ragged volley sounded and the 18-pounder, overlooking the southeast corner of the fort, fired. Travis broke into a trot with Brown right behind him. Shouting and firing rang out on the south wall, and the cannons of the Mexicans responded with a barrage that threw dirt and stone all over the central plaza. Travis dived for cover near the barracks, got up, and dodged his way to the palisade with Brown still following.

Massed near the crest of the hills that flanked the fort were thousands of Mexican soldiers, their banners flapping in the late evening breeze and their armor flashing orange in the setting sun. Crockett and his Tennesseans stood watching, much like men waiting for the beginning of a parade. Two of Brown's men had climbed into firing position and were using their ART-scoped M-14's, trying to kill the officers.

There was another barrage from the Mexican artillery, and everyone scrambled for cover as the cannonballs thudded against the side of the chapel. The Mexican band began Deguello again and there was a rising shout as the mass on the hill began to spread and run down the slopes, funneling itself toward the short fence being guarded by only thirty men.

Travis ran to the corner of the chapel's plaza and shouted at the roof-top battery. "Fire. FIRE!"

Brown stepped to the palisade and unslung his rifle. He flipped the safety off, aimed, and fired. All along the wall the others did the same, and Mexican soldiers began to drop out of the formation.

Travis ran to Brown and tapped his shoulder. "You take over here. I've got to get to my battle station."

Brown nodded without looking back. Travis took off at a dead run, shouting a warning to the rest of the garrison, in case they weren't aware that the fight was on. He passed Bromhead who, with 15 others, stood with their rifles held at high port, bayonets fixed. Bromhead expected to be needed on the south wall and was closest to it, but he could hit any hole in the defense.

The firing grew in intensity until it was a continual roar. From the parapet near the palisade, Brown heard one of the recoilless rifles open fire. Dirt mushroomed and Mexicans died, but they kept coming, returning fire.

Then, to the east, another Mexican battery opened fire. On the chapel roof, Bonham tried to turn his cannon, but the mount was stuck. Dennison and Waters grabbed the recoilless rifle, jerked it out of the tripod, and started down the ladder. Waters yelled over his shoulder, "I got the mount. Someone bring the ammo."

They scrambled across the courtyard, through the chapel doors, and ran up the ramp. Another volley was fired at them and slammed into the chapel walls. Flying stone clipped a number of the men there, and a fist-sized rock hit a Texan just below the right eye. The Texan took two staggering steps backward and toppled over the wall, falling twelve feet to the ground outside the fort.

Waters and Dennison set up the recoilless rifle, slammed

a round into it, and fired. It was short, but only by a couple of yards. The Mexicans there swarmed over the protective earthworks, looking for cover.

Waters shouted at Crawford. "Get our ammo. Quick."

Crawford had been standing at the bottom of the ramp. He sprinted out the door and was gone for only seconds. He came back, with McGee and Wolfe behind him, carrying armloads of the ammunition.

Both McGee and Wolfe dropped the ammo in a pile. McGee said, "We've got to get back."

Waters nodded absently, stripping the protective sleeves off the rounds. He crammed one into the weapon and Dennison fired it. They hit the earthwork in front of an enemy cannon, but didn't destroy the weapon.

"Damn." Dennison adjusted the sights.

"Don't worry, we'll get it."

Dennison looked over the weapon at Waters. "That's not it. I didn't want to get involved in a counter-battery duel. They're tying up our artillery while it should be blasting holes in their lines."

In the south, the heavy firing caught the Mexicans by surprise and they veered to their left, hitting the south wall in front of the barracks, but well away from the palisade. Suddenly the Texans' weapons were no good. The Mexicans were jammed against the wall, and it was not possible to fire directly into the Mexican troops because the wall was too thick. They couldn't fire over the top of it without exposing themselves to the Mexican sharpshooters who were stationed in the rear of the battalions to protect the assault troops.

Movement to his right caught Brown's eye and he looked in time to see one of his snipers, Jim Stewart, fall from the parapet above him. When he looked back, he saw that the Mexicans had thrown up their scaling ladders and were fighting their way to the top. There was a final volley from the Mexican sharpshooters to clear the top of the wall, and then the enemy was there, trying to swarm over onto the parapets.

The defenders leaped to meet them, and for an instant the fighting was hand to hand on the wall, bayonet against Bowie knife, musket against long rifle, and man against man.

One group of Mexicans, with a huge battering ram, tried to smash the small gate in the center of the south wall but were unsuccessful. They had already captured the Texas artillery that guarded the door and had killed the gun crew. While an officer shouted instructions, the men loaded one of the cannons and spun it around until it was pointing directly at the gate. The Texans on the wall had to keep their heads down or have them shot off; so they didn't know what was happening at the foot of the wall.

Brown, on the other hand, knew exactly what was happening. He had studied the history of the battle as outlined in the briefing packet Millsaps had given him. He looked at Bromhead but decided that it wasn't time to commit the tiny reserve. Instead he yelled to his troops, "Come on. Follow me." He knew that Crockett's men would stay at the palisade until Crockett told them to move.

The mercenaries fell away from the palisade, grouped near Brown, and then took off at a dead run for the southwest corner of the fort. They split into small groups to clamor up the ladders that the Texans had placed there earlier. Three of them were running past the south gate when the Mexicans fired the cannon. The blast ripped though the flimsy wood of the gate and hit the men, crushing them to the ground and rolling them over. Bob Crossman was knocked down by the concussion, but not his two friends, Tony Wolfe and Joe Hawkins. Both were hit by wood splinters and grapeshot, and both died as they touched the ground.

Crossman scrambled on his hands and knees over to the

Texas battery that guarded the inside of the gate. The men manning it were afraid to use it for fear of killing Texans, but Crossman didn't have that problem with his Ingram. The first Mexicans through the gate died in a hail of bullets. While Crossman reloaded, the Texans used their long rifles, and between them, they kept the bodies piling up in the narrow gateway.

On the parapets, there were so many men crammed together, no one could use his rifle or musket. Brown jerked at his holster and pulled out his Browning. He grabbed hold of a Mexican rifle barrel with his hand as the enemy soldier tried to bayonet him, pulled it forward, and twisted the muzzle of his pistol into the man's stomach. He fired once, and the Mexican fell backward.

The confusion increased. Brown wanted to get out of the open, but there was nowhere to go. He kept his eyes moving. With the edge of the parapet at his back and the wall in front of him, the enemy couldn't get behind him, but more of them were reaching the top of the wall, gaining the parapet. Using his pistol carefully, he managed to shoot three more.

The jam at the foot of the wall continued to grow, and the Mexicans, rather than push forward, began to edge along the wall, eventually reaching the palisade. They hit it on the southwest corner, using part of the Alamo wall for cover.

Brown saw what was happening and realized that it was one of the compromising changes that history would make. In the first battle, the Mexicans had steered well clear of Crockett's corner of the Alamo because the losses had been so heavy, but they had also gotten over the south wall. Now they had had time to re-evaluate and capitalize on an advantage.

The right side of the palisade began to collapse almost as soon as the Mexicans attacked it. They poured over, backing Crockett and his men toward the chapel, forcing them to abandon their cannon. Brown turned and moved closer to the flying squad standing below him. He yelled, "Bromhead."

Bromhead glanced up, saw where Brown was pointing, and shouted over his shoulder, "Follow me."

He took two steps and was shot in the face by a Mexican marksman. Bromhead staggered and collapsed in the dust. Thompson took over, leading the rest to the palisade.

Brown watched for a moment too long and, as he turned, a Mexican soldier hit him in the head with a rifle butt. Brown pitched backward off the parapet, unconscious.

The battle now degenerated into individual conflicts. Thompson and her force caught the Mexicans at the palisade completely by surprise. They waded in, using their bayonets and rifles. As the Mexicans turned to meet them, Crockett saw his opportunity and attacked. They split the Mexicans into groups. One was trying to get back over the palisade, hoping to escape for a moment, while the others were forced across the chapel courtyard, trying to take cover in the ground floor of the hospital.

Crockett and his men forced the Mexicans into the hospital and then went in after them. The long dark room was sparsely furnished and offered little cover. In the far corner, the Mexicans fanned out in a ring, daring Crockett and his men to come after them. While part of them guarded, the rest rapidly reloaded. Sporadic firing rippled. Crockett and a few of his men dodged to the side, tipping beds over. One or two were hit and fell.

The Mexicans, seeing the advantage, began an advance, ignoring the narrow stairs used by Mary Jo and the medics to evacuate seconds earlier, but it was cut short. The door crashed open and one of the mercenaries dived in, rolled to his side and came up firing. He emptied one magazine, jerked it out of the weapon, and jammed in another. But it was unnecessary; the enemy had been killed.

Crockett helped the mercenary to his feet and said, "I don't know what kind of rifle you have, but it sure is impressive."

The Mexicans were now pouring over the palisade, trying to reach the inner courtyard so that they could break the defense on the parapets. Along with several of the men, Thompson was pushed back until she bumped against the adobe walls of the rooms on the south side of the courtyard. With her bayonet, she held the Mexicans at bay. Once she had to pull the trigger of her M-14 because the bayonet had gotten stuck between a Mexican's ribs. The blast and recoil loosened it enough to pull free.

Three Mexican soldiers came at her at once, two with bayonets and the third with his sword. She lunged at one, but he pushed her bayonet to the side with his rifle. The swordsman grabbed the barrel of her rifle with his free hand and jerked it away from her. One of the bayonet men tried to kill her, but she ducked under his slashing cut, struggling to draw her pistol. The swordsman had dropped her rifle and was now trying to decapitate her. She kicked upward, hitting him in the crotch. He fell to his knees, ignoring everything else.

Thompson dropped backward, trying desperately to get away from the other two men. They pressed forward as she got her pistol clear of the holster. She shot one of them in the head, dodged around a bayonet thrust, and pumped three bullets into the chest of the other man.

Near her, Sammy Blair was surrounded by Mexicans. He had given up the art of bayonet and was swinging his rifle like a baseball bat. The Mexicans were trying to duck under his swings, but weren't having much luck.

Thompson watched for a moment, evaluating the situation, and then forced her way toward him, shooting two of the enemy. Blair then began easing backward, trying to withdraw far enough so that he could reverse his grip on the rifle.

About this time, Crockett's men, having cleared the ground floor of the hospital, appeared in the doorway. They didn't push their way out, but took up firing positions, trying to kill the enemy as they scrambled over the palisade. The added firepower momentarily confused the Mexicans. Thompson used the moment to climb the short wall that separated the chapel courtyard from the rest of the plaza. When the courtyard was cleared of Mexicans, other than the dead and dying, Crockett and his men ran back to the palisade. Thompson and the mercenaries fell in with them, keeping the enemy away from that part of the fort.

On the parapets, the decisive battle was being fought. With Brown either dead or wounded, no one knew which, command of the mercenaries fell to Jim McGee. He was standing on the southwest corner of the parapet, trying to keep the Mexicans from using their scaling ladders. As an enemy soldier reached the top of the wall, McGee would either bayonet or club him, and then push the ladder away from the wall. His back was being guarded by three of his friends.

All three were using their bayonets, dodging and weaving, avoiding the enemy's weapons and killing with their own. James Garret was pushed backward by two Mexicans. As he took a final step, he twisted his ankle because he hadn't seen a rifle lying under his feet. He tried to regain his balance by throwing out his right hand, but that left his chest uncovered. A Mexican thrust with a bayonet, but the chest protector of Garret's bulletproof vest stopped the blow. Garret grabbed the soldier's rifle barrel and the Mexican jerked it back, pulling Garret with it. The other Mexican lunged forward, the tip of his bayonet ripping into Garret's throat. He looked surprised and then angered as he fell.

Bill Linn saw it all happen. He pushed forward, clubbed a Mexican soldier to his knees, and then slashed his throat as he moved. Linn came up behind the other two before they could turn. He smashed one in the back of the head with the butt of his rifle and continued the motion so that he hit the other man just above the ear. He spun in time to see McGee drop to the ground and sprint up the ramp of the 18-pounder next to them.

McGee, using part of the barricade at the top of the dirt ramp for cover, and still using single shot, was trying to kill all the Mexicans before they could get over the wall so that they couldn't reinforce the men who had now gained a shaky foothold there.

The artillerymen had turned the cannon so that it faced the in-coming enemy and were stuffing the barrel with anything they could find, including the ejected cartridges of McGee's weapon. They fired once, clearing the enemy from the southwest corner of the fort, but that drew a concentrated return fire. Two of the Alamo defenders fell, one over the barrel of the cannon, the other, one of Brown's mercenaries, Willis Moore, rolled down the slope.

The fighting on the parapet was slowly being won by the Mexicans because of their numbers. Now they were too close so that any advantage of using the automatic weapons, brought by Brown's mercenaries, was negated. No one could open fire without shooting half a dozen friends. McGee, having seen this, shouted over the firing, "Abandon the wall. Fall back. FALL BACK!"

A few of the men near him heard the shouts and tried to ease their way off the parapet calling to the others to fall back. Slowly the word spread as the men of the Alamo tried to escape from the tide of Mexicans. It began to look as if Brown had overplayed his hand, as if the mercenaries had blown it, giving the victory to the enemy.

One by one, the men dropped off the parapet and sprinted for cover in the buildings along the west wall, at the battery inside the walls, or behind the low wall that separated the main plaza from the chapel courtyard. The Mexicans used the short walls at the top of the parapets for cover and were shooting at anyone they could see. The Texans on the west wall made good targets, and the toll there was so high that they almost abandoned their posts. There wasn't much of an assault hitting the west wall, but if the defense collapsed, the Mexicans would swarm over the wall.

McGee decided that the time had come. They had waited, just as Brown had wanted, but no more Mr. Nice Guy. McGee scrambled around near the 18-pounder, searching for the firing control for the claymores. A thousand or more Mexicans were now herded against the base of the south wall, waiting for a chance to climb the scaling ladders.

McGee found the control and hit the buttons. There was a series of small explosions as the claymores fired, showering the Mexicans from behind with thousands of steel balls. All along the south wall, Mexicans died. The attack from the rear totally confused the men there. Those who hadn't been killed or seriously wounded suddenly broke to the left and right, running to get out of the way of this new attack. They didn't stay to reinforce their fellow soldiers who had won the parapets, but left them there to die.

As soon as he had fired the claymores, McGee switched to full automatic, sweeping the nearest buildings with quick deadly bursts. Mexicans fell in bunches, many wounded, but even more dead. From the plaza, the mercenaries followed McGee's lead and went to full automatic, raking the whole south wall. One or two of them threw grenades as fast as they could pull the pins. Within seconds, there were only dead or dying Mexicans there, and the defenders reclaimed the parapets, pushed the scaling ladders to the ground, and fired a few shots at the distant backs of the fleeing troops.

From the collapse of the south wall until its total recapture and the breaking of the assault, only a minute and a half had passed.

On the north wall, Travis and his men had their hands full, but the fighting was not nearly as fierce as it had been in the south. Most of the column that hit the west wall had diverted to the north, as did the column on the east. While those three columns totalled less than the one that attacked the south, the force was large enough to take the fort, if they could get in.

Travis had taken complete command of the north wall. He tried to synchronize the firing of the rifles so that a steady stream of rifle shot, along with grape from the cannon, would be pouring into the Mexican lines.

The first attack hesitated at the wide stream that they had to cross, and while they worked at it, the Texans tore holes in the Mexican formations. Dozens of soldiers dropped into the water, and in the scramble to find some cover, most of the scaling ladders were lost. On the Alamo side of the stream, Mexican officers organized a brief attack, but the soldiers were so vulnerable to the deadly fire from the Texans, that the assault broke before it had carried very far. In the end, it was almost a rout, the Mexicans stampeding in an attempt to get to safety.

But they didn't stay away very long. Insulted by their officers, who were screaming that the men in the south were still fighting and dying, the Mexicans roared forward again, crossed the stream quickly, and succeeded in reaching the north wall.

The Texas firing was so heavy, however, that the assault began to waver. With their scaling ladders gone, they had no way of climbing the walls. They moved toward the breach and began clawing at the rubble thrown into it, trying to find a way into the fort.

Travis was busy trying to keep his men firing in volleys. With the majority of Mexican soldiers scattering, he didn't notice those who were trying to get through the breach. There was little resistance, and with very little effort, a handful of Mexicans found themselves standing inside the Alamo. The defenders had their backs to them.

The Mexicans spread out, first looking for cover. Then they began to fire at the defenders, confusing them, and causing them to dive for cover. The enemy outside, seeing the walls partially abandoned, scrambled to find their ladders or anything else that would help them scale the walls.

Andy Kent and Bob Cunningham were standing in the northeast corner of the fort. When they realized what was happening, they both fell to their stomachs and crawled to the edge of the parapet. That offered them some cover, and they opened fire, raking the plaza, with their 9-mm submachine guns.

For a moment, everyone, Texan and Mexican, was pinned down. But then the Mexicans began to climb over the wall. Kent rolled to his side and fired on full automatic. The Mexicans who had been unfortunate enough to get to the top, fell off, dead or wounded.

Kent crawled back to the wall and tried to peek over the top, but couldn't see anything. Outside there were hundreds of bugle calls and a thousand voices shouting. Behind him, he heard Cunningham's weapon chattering.

Then, from somewhere below him, along the inside of the east wall, he heard a shout that grew into a roar. He looked back and saw the Texans, led by Travis, charge across the plaza.

More of the enemy tried to get through the breach, but some of those with Travis turned to meet them. The fighting was hand to hand. Travis had thrown away his double-barrelled shotgun after firing both barrels. He used his sword, chopping through the Mexicans as if they were tall grass blocking his path. Two or three Mexicans raised rifles to shoot him, but their aim was bad or Travis was faster. He killed one and chased the others from their cover.

Cunningham clamored to his knees and then dropped from the parapet, running to the ramp of the cannon there. While the Texans chased the Mexicans back through the breach, or kicked in the doors of the rooms on the west wall, searching for stragglers, Cunningham used his Ingram to keep the enemy away from the breach. Kent was now standing, bent slightly so that he wasn't too exposed, and was pouring lead into the Mexican ranks. Both of them were joined by Texans who had abandoned their positions as it began to look like the Mexicans were going to take the north wall.

The firing seemed to slowly increase in intensity. The Texans were working as fast as they could, reloading their weapons. The cannons fired almost continuously, tearing huge holes in the Mexican formations. There was a momentary rising shout from the Mexicans and a brief surge forward, but it was only the last gasp. They reached the foot of the wall once more, but the scaling ladders were gone, and the breach was plugged by two dozen Texans. There was no place for them to go.

They fell back slowly as the Texans continued to inflict heavy losses. When they were out of range, Travis shouted for a cease fire, and was greeted with silence. The attack on the south wall had been broken minutes earlier, and the firing there had died to the occasional sniper's rifle shot from the mercenaries. There was only the heavy smoke that drifted to the east, and the silence that covered all.

TWENTY-SEVEN

The men in the Alamo waited quietly, expecting another assault because the Mexicans had been inside the fort and it was only by good luck and automatic weapons that they had been forced out. Travis kept his men at their battle stations throughout the oncoming dusk, until it was too dark to see anything. Outside the fort, they could hear the screams of the wounded and the rattling of equipment as Mexican doctors moved through the battlefield trying to help those that still lived.

In the distance there was more noise that sounded as if the Mexican army was pulling out, but Travis didn't believe it. He knew they had hurt Santa Anna, but he didn't think they had crushed him. At 8:30 Travis ordered half the men off the walls to eat and catch some sleep.

By 10:00, the moon was up, throwing its bright white light over the battlefield and revealing downtown Bexar. The blood-red banner that had stood over the Military Plaza for 12 days was gone. The town was without light.

The cantinas, where Mexican officers had tried to impress and entertain Mexican girls, were all dark. The music that had drifted to the Alamo for 12 nights was now silent.

All of which worried Travis. He hadn't expected Santa Anna to give up so easily. It was true that within the fort there were over four-hundred Mexican casualties, including dead, wounded, or captured; but that was less than ten percent of the estimated force. Outside there were more but Travis couldn't believe they had destroyed Santa Anna. Travis called for Jim Bonham and Charlie Baker. Both men were told to ride out, scout the local territory for twenty minutes, and report back immediately. If something was brewing, Travis wanted to know what.

By midnight, Bonham and Baker returned to report that the Mexicans had pulled out. Their cannon emplacements were abandoned, their tents had vanished, and Bonham had boldly walked into the house that had been Santa Anna's new headquarters during the siege. There were still maps tacked to the walls, papers scattered on the floor, with one dead officer in the hallway, but no trace of Santa Anna's staff or of the generalissimo, himself.

Travis listened quietly, letting no emotion show on his face, although he was slowly beginning to believe that the Texas War for Independence had been won. He pointed to John Baugh. "John, I want you to round up the officers, including Crockett and Brown."

"Colonel Brown has been wounded, though not badly."

"Well, if he can't make it, then send one of his people. Tell them we'll meet here in fifteen minutes and then I'll speak to the garrison. Tell Bowie what's happened and see if he is up to being carried out for the meeting."

Baugh saluted as he said, "Yes, sir," and turned toward the door. He stopped with his hand on the knob. "You don't think it's over, do you, Will?"

"I don't know. I hope so, but I don't know."

Travis told his officers both what he had heard and what he believed. He knew that the Mexicans had pulled far back, but he didn't really think they had abandoned their effort to recapture the Alamo. Santa Anna had thousands of men strung out in a column that was working its way north. He might have retreated only long enough for those men, some of them the cream of his army, to catch up. Travis proposed that they remain in the Alamo until ordered out. He was going to tell the same thing to the men. Without another word, and without asking for anyone's opinion, he stood and then moved to the door before saying, "Please fall in with your men."

A chilly wind had picked up, blowing clouds by the moon. In the flickering light of campfires and torches, Travis could see the majority of his command. Only twenty-three had been killed during the battle, most of them on the south wall. He studied the tired men for a minute, letting the drama build as they awaited the official word. Rumors had swept through the fort for the last hour, including one that Fannin had driven the Mexicans out of Bexar.

As the men quieted, Travis began his speech. He clasped his hands behind his back and strolled in front of them. "Jim Bonham and Charlie Baker returned a little while ago. I had sent them out to inspect the surrounding area. It would seem that Santa Anna has withdrawn."

There was silence for a moment, and then suddenly cheering. Men jumped up and down and swatted each other on the back. Some laughed and a few cried. One or two began singing and Travis yelled for them to be quiet, but it had little effect. It was like Christmas and a first love all rolled into one and, after 12 days of near hopeless siege, the men couldn't help reacting with pure joy. Travis gave up trying to quiet them and waited.

When the men had finally worn themselves down, Travis said, "But, I'm afraid that he has merely gone to join forces with the rest of his army. Until morning, we can't be sure how decisive our victory has been."

For several minutes, Travis tried to explain the situation. As he had said at the beginning of the siege, he couldn't see Santa Anna bypassing that many armed men, especially since they had defeated him once. Until Houston contacted them to relieve them, he felt it was their duty to remain in the Alamo. Naturally, the regulars would have to stay with him, but the majority of the command was made up of volunteers.

Travis pulled his sword from the scabbard and drew a long line in the dirt. "We've had extremely good luck until now and I hope that it will hold. I don't expect to be here much longer, but I will stay forever if I am so ordered to. However, you men have done what has been asked of you. You have fought the Mexicans here and you have inflicted penalties upon them, giving Houston the time he needs. No one will think less of you if you decide to return to your homes and families. I ask those of you who will stay with me to cross the line." Travis stepped back to wait.

Jim Bowie, sick with fever and practically dead of disease, raised himself shakily to one elbow and said, "Would a couple of you boys help me across? Me and Will have a job to do."

One of the men looked at him. "I don't know, Jim. I think I might just head on home."

Another man pushed the first one out of the way. "Then move aside. I'll help him over, and I'll stay."

Jim Bonham moved to the other side, helped to lift Bowie, and then helped walk him across the line. "I'll stay as long as you say, Will."

Slowly the men moved across the line, forming a rank to the rear of Travis, until only the mercenaries and one

Alamo defender remained behind. Davy Crockett looked at the man and said, "Come on, Louie. Make it over here."

Louis Rose took a step forward and then stopped. "No. I think that it is time to leave. I learned that when I fought in France. When it's time to get out, it's time to get out."

Travis put his sword back in the scabbard. "How about you and your men, Colonel Brown?"

"We've done our job by breaking Santa Anna's back. There are other places we're needed." Brown had a headache from his wound but on the whole felt good.

Although he felt no loyalty to the corporation after the lies that they had told, he said, "You might consider mounting an expedition into northern Mexico. That would certainly end this."

Travis took a step toward Brown. "I don't think Sam Houston would approve of such a tactic."

"Colonel Travis." It was Millsaps, who had been hiding in the chapel during the fighting. He had agreed with the others to stay in 1836, but he still wanted to do what he could for Texas-American, feeling that they might take care of his family. "If I may be so bold as to suggest something. I have studied military tactics extensively," he lied, "and I have found that the best defense is an offense. If you were to mount an operation to Matamores, it would keep the Mexicans so busy that they wouldn't have a chance to attack Texas again."

Bonham interrupted. "I've just come from Goliad, where the remains of the first invasion reported. The Mexicans stopped them short of their goal and chopped them up badly. An attack on Matamores wouldn't work. In fact, it hasn't."

Travis looked toward Bonham and then back to Millsaps. He said, simply, "That is not my duty. Gentlemen, please get back to your posts. Mr. Rose, I'd like to talk to you briefly before you go."

As the formation began to break up, the men walking slowly toward the darkened parts of the fort, Millsaps moved to Travis and took his sleeve to stop him. Even though Travis looked at him like a mess the dog had left, Millsaps said, "Colonel, I wasn't suggesting that you leave your post. Only that you say something to Houston. Hell, maybe you and Fannin could mount such an attack."

"Shut up, Millsaps," said Brown as he stepped closer to the corporate man. "Colonel Travis has more important things on his mind." Brown grabbed Millsaps' arm and jerked him away from Travis as he said, "I'm sorry about this."

"Don't let it bother you. Many volunteers have delusions of grandeur."

"Yes, but some of them may deserve to feel that way. Millsaps is just a dumb son of a bitch."

Travis smiled, probably for the first time in days. "Your estimate of him may be somewhat generous." He turned and headed for the Alamo headquarters.

It wasn't until shortly before 2:00 in the morning of March 6 that Brown and his mercenaries were ready to leave. According to the corporate instructions, with which Brown agreed, they were to pick up anything that could be identified as modern. They were to leave nothing behind, and Brown tried to get it all. Naturally, they had lost a large number of shell casings, especially after the firefight near the sugar mill, but that couldn't be helped. Brown, however, didn't want to leave behind a flashlight, or wristwatch, or submachine gun.

Travis had ordered a number of men to help Brown and his people get their horses ready and carefully packed. When they had finished, Travis walked over. The moon threw a cold light on the scene. The group stood clustered near the south gate. Bodies had been pulled out of the way, but many still lay scattered on the parapets, the cannon emplacements and around the courtyard.

After checking several of the pack animals, Brown called to Travis. "I guess that about does it."

Brown looked at the mounted figures of his force. They all sat quietly, waiting for him to give the orders to move out. Brown wanted to leave, thought that it was best. History would record the group of men who rode into the Alamo on March 1, and in fact, had. Now they were leaving as a body so that the real defenders wouldn't have a chance to wonder about them. The story of going to find Houston was thin, but it was, at least, moderately believable.

While he hesitated, he took another look around the Alamo. It was just as it had appeared the first night, except now there were nearly five-hundred dead men lying under the bright stars. As a soldier, Brown knew that he wasn't supposed to feel emotion about the dead, especially enemy dead, but these had been brave men. All of them. Texan and Mexicans, all were brave. He hated to leave. Hated to leave this tall thin man in the outlandish costume. Brown didn't really like Travis, but he now respected him as a fellow soldier. Brown shook Travis' hand. It was like shaking hands with history. "Good luck, Will."

Someone opened the gate. Brown climbed into the saddle, turned to look at his force, and then threw a salute at Travis. He spurred his horse, ducked under the arch and was outside the Alamo. He turned left, angled for the road to Gonzales, and then looked back one last time. The Alamo was quiet.

TWENTY-EIGHT

A sliver of red in the east suggested that dawn was close as the mercenaries halted on a grassy hilltop about fifteen miles from the Alamo. Off to the right, a single thunderstorm tried to pour itself into the ground with continuous flashes of lightning and an ominous rumbling that sounded like all of Santa Anna's cannons firing at once.

Brown slid out of his saddle, and then patted the horse on the flank as he moved toward the others. As he stared at the six poncho-covered bodies, he said, "Some of you grab the shovels. This is the spot."

Silently the mercenaries dismounted. A half-dozen of them pulled entrenching tools from the pack animals while Brown directed the rest. They gently lifted the bodies off the horses and lined them up near a huge oak tree. The only noise was the raspy scrape of the shovels and an occasional blast of thunder. No one spoke.

The sky slowly brightened, the sun forcing back the darkness. Brown watched the holes deepen and finally said, "All right, that's enough."

Without a word, the men and women who had been digging climbed up while the remainder picked up the bodies and carried them closer to the holes. Brown nodded and they carefully lowered the bodies into the graves.

It took only a few minutes to cover the dead. As they packed down the dirt, Brown said, "We'd better cover them with rocks to stop scavengers. Then I'll say some words."

When they were done, they stepped back and waited. Brown pulled off his hat and gazed at the six rock-covered mounds. "I've done this a dozen times," he said, "and watched it done a hundred more, but the words never seem right. I could tell you that we all met only a few short weeks ago and that together we have participated in a unique experience, but you know that. Anything I could say would only seem hollow and insincere."

He paused, looking into the faces of the survivors. "We all lost friends. Maybe they died because there was nothing better waiting for them. But, at least they had some choice in the matter, and that makes them luckier than most. We won't forget them."

Again he stopped and glanced toward the beacon that the Texas-American Oil Company had given them. It was strapped to one of the pack horses. It had a sand-bagged base to give it stability, and its bright-blue flashing light could be used as a rally point for the mercenaries after dark. Brown had never thought to ask Millsaps for the code after they had made the decision to stay in the past. Since Millsaps wasn't part of the fighting force, it had never occurred to Brown that Millsaps could be killed and the secret die with him, although that didn't make any difference. They weren't going to use the beacon anyway.

There didn't seem to be anything more to say. Brown moved to the pack horse and unloaded the beacon. He found the switch that controlled the blue rally light and flipped it. All eyes were on him as he set it in the center of the graves. He stepped back and stared at it, but could think of no more words.

For a moment he watched the blue light flashing off the tree, the mounds of rock, and the men and women standing at the graves. Finally he put on his cap. "There's nothing more to do here. Let's go."

Slowly, after they had finished paying individual respects, they climbed on their horses and left, singly or in two's and three's. Most didn't look back.

Brown watched them leave, wondering what most of them would do. They had never discussed that, never had the chance. He supposed that some of them would look for Sam Houston and go on to fight at San Jacinto. Others would probably ride back to the United States and set themselves up for life. As he had said, there were a thousand ways for bright, knowledgeable people to make a fortune in the land of opportunity. Brown hadn't decided where to invest his money. He just knew that he was going to do it in Philadelphia for the time being.

From behind him, he heard Thompson say, "Hadn't we better go?"

"There's no real hurry."

"What about the Mexicans? You know as well as I do that we didn't really crush Santa Anna. He still has the majority of his army and there are probably patrols all around us."

"Sure. But Santa Anna has retreated to the south, to rejoin his forces and lick his wounded ego. It'll be a week or more before he can do anything. As for patrols, while I suppose there will be some, they'll be guarding the main body and won't roam too far afield. I doubt that we have to worry about them being around here."

Thompson didn't say anything more. She climbed into the saddle and waited quietly, watching the blue light spin its slow circle. Overhead the clouds seemed to be gathering, not for rain or snow, but only to darken the sky, and she thought that it seemed fitting that the sky should reflect the mood.

She turned back to the beacon and then smiled. It would be ironic if Texas-American tried to initiate a recall without a signal from the mercenaries! Instead of retrieving the survivors, they'd get the bodies and the beacon and never know what had happened.

Brown glanced up toward her as he grabbed the reins of his horse. "Now it's time."

Half-way down the hill, he stopped. Placing a hand on the horse's flank, he turned to look back. The beacon was still there, silently flashing past the tree, lighting the bottom branches, showering the graves in a brief blue glow, and then whipping back to the tree. It was a fitting marker. Something that would stump anyone who came upon it. He didn't know how long the batteries would last; but the country was desolate and sparsely populated, so it could be years before anyone found the graves. It didn't matter. He had said goodbye and left a suitable marker. He dug his heels into the horse's flanks and started off again. Thompson followed closely. It was all over.

HISTORICAL PERSPECTIVE:

March 5, 1836, would become the red letter day in the battle of the Alamo. Santa Anna suddenly knew that the final assault had to take place on the morning of the sixth. The threat of Fannin and his four-hundred men in Goliad was too great. Santa Anna had to take the Alamo before those reinforcements could arrive, bringing more cannon and powder.

Santa Anna called his staff together, asking them what they thought about an all-out assault. Most of them hesitated, wanting to wait for the rest of the Mexican army that was bringing larger cannons. Only one officer pushed for the attack as soon as it could be organized. He pointed out that the Mexican army had already suffered enough humiliation at the hands of the rebellious Texans and it was time to teach them all a lesson. Santa Anna finally became impatient with the bickering, chased all the officers out, and made the decision himself. He would attack just as soon as he could get everything organized and his troops back into position.

Under the cover of darkness, Santa Anna positioned his men. They quietly slipped into a loose ring, hoping to cut off all escape from the Alamo. By 4:00, all the assault troops were on line and waiting.

Inside the Alamo, Travis sat writing another message to Fannin, describing all that had happened. James Allen was selected to carry it. He rode bareback and had no trouble with Mexican patrols.

By 4:00 everything was quiet in the Alamo. A few tired men had been stationed outside the walls in case the Mexicans tried a sneak attack. Inside, only one man, J.J. Baugh, was awake. He was slowly patrolling, watching, and waiting, not really expecting anything.

Halicar, HISTORIAN
First Assistant to the Chief Archivist

TWENTY-NINE

Captain John Baugh, Travis' adjutant, had pulled the night duty for what little of the night was left. He had been there when Brown and the mercenaries rode out. He had given the order to close the gate as Travis slowly walked back to the Alamo headquarters.

He was making his rounds, checking the outposts, the sentries, and what little movement he could see. Outside the walls there seemed to be none. The moon had dropped toward the western horizon, and high scattered clouds blocked out the starlight making it hard to see very far. San Antonio was dark, as were the hillsides surrounding it. Baugh was uneasy because he felt the battle had been too simple. He couldn't believe that Santa Anna would withdraw even with the heavy losses he had suffered. Baugh was afraid of Santa Anna. He knew of Santa Anna's temper and his ruthlessness. The blood-red banner that had flown above the Military Plaza had not been an idle threat.

Baugh strolled up the dirt ramp that led to the battery on

the center of the north wall, near the breach. Green Jameson and the Alamo engineers had tried to close the hole, but the work was rough and unfinished. Baugh stared into the darkness.

For a moment Baugh stood with one foot on a spoke of the cannon's wheel. He took a paper and tobacco out of his pocket and rolled a cigarette. He didn't light it, just hung onto it, saving it until he was safely away from the battery's powder supply. There was nothing for him to see.

At the bottom of the ramp, he lit the cigarette and puffed deeply. Outside the fort he thought he heard a voice and turned to look, although all he could see was the cannon and the wall. There was another shout, and then another, and suddenly, it sounded as if there were thousands of men yelling out there in the dark. Baugh tossed the cigarette away and ran back up the ramp. Now there were bugles and a band playing.

Santa Anna could wait no longer. He had ordered the attack.

Baugh's first reaction was that it was a trick. Then he thought it was another harassment raid; but as the noise grew and firing broke out from Mexican positions that Baugh had thought were abandoned, he turned. There was no word from the sentries posted outside the walls. That could only mean they had already been overrun.

Baugh sprinted down the ramp and ran toward the Alamo headquarters, shouting, "Colonel Travis. Colonel Travis. The Mexicans are coming."

Travis appeared in the doorway of his headquarters before Baugh could reach it. In one hand he held his double-barrelled shotgun and in the other his sword. The question in his eyes died as he heard the shouting and shooting going on beyond the wall. He waved once, and Baugh spun to follow him as he ran to the north wall.

There was no need to give orders. The surprised defenders opened fire as targets appeared. Next to Travis, one of the cannons roared and then the other. Firing broke out on the west wall as an assault force loomed out of the dark bank of the San Antonio River.

Cannon fire poured out of the Alamo, tearing huge holes in the Mexican lines. The column attacking from the north was driven back before they could reach the wall. They never planted their scaling ladders and, in fact, lost most of them before they crossed the stream.

The columns attacking from the east and west had little better luck. They reached the fort but that was all. The fire from the Texans' long rifles and the grapeshot from the cannons were far too deadly.

In the south, the Mexicans thought that the palisade defended by Crockett would be easy to storm. The first wave headed straight for it and was met with such heavy and accurate firing, they had to bear to the left. The column reached the walls on the south, planted their ladders, and a few brave men tried to climb them. They died in the attempt, and the attack was beaten back.

It took only minutes for the Mexicans to regroup. Again, from all four sides they attacked, but the men in the east column broke to their right while those in the west broke left and both groups ended on the north side of the Alamo. The northern column, fighting the heavy fire from the fort was suddenly reinforced. They pushed forward, falling in behind the mass of men that had accidentally found the north wall.

The men of the east and west two columns, taking the brunt of the Texas guns, tried to retreat; but the northern column forced them forward, and they reached the base of the walls. Somewhere they found a couple of the scaling ladders and planted them, but they were quickly pushed back. None of the Mexicans tried to climb up. The assault had failed a second time.

Again, it was on the south wall where the fighting was the heaviest. That column, realizing that they would never reach the palisade guarded by Crockett, didn't even attack it. They hit the wall on the southwestern corner, planted their ladders, and started climbing. This time they reached the top where Texans jumped to meet them in hand-to-hand fighting on the yard-wide wall. Most of the enemy were shot, clubbed, or stabbed before they could gain a foothold. One or two may have managed to get into the fort, but they died before they could cause any serious trouble. The assault was finally repulsed.

For a few minutes, the Mexicans rested. Santa Anna, realizing that his current strategy was costing him the cream of his army, decided that he would mass the troops for an assault on the north. To insure their success, he committed his tiny reserve.

He also realized that there was only one more attack possible. His men had taken too much of a beating already that morning, and if they failed a third time, they wouldn't be pushed into a fourth. He would have to wait for the siege cannon that were still inching their way northward with the remainder of his army. He would lose precious time, time that the Texans needed to form their rebel army. Everything was riding on the third assault.

The attack came quickly. One massive column hit the north wall, while a small force attacked the western end of the southern wall. For the third time, the Mexicans reached it, placed their ladders, and started up. For the third time, the Texans were ready, brushing aside bayonets with tomahawks and knives. The Mexicans wavered but endured, fighting for a toehold.

The decisive battle, however, was taking place on the north wall. Travis was directing the cannon fire, hoping to keep the Mexicans away from the breach. He saw a group trying to place a ladder and, leaning over the wall, discharged one barrel of his shotgun at them. At almost the same instant, a Mexican rifleman fired, and the round grazed Travis in the head. He dropped his shotgun amid the Mexican force below him, staggered back, and rolled down the ramp. He ended in a sitting position at the base of the ramp, dazed but conscious.

The Mexicans under the north wall couldn't move. There were too many men behind them, forcing them forward, giving them no choice but to climb the walls or be crushed. They clawed at the rubble tossed into the breach, scrambled over it, and were surprised to find themselves suddenly inside the Alamo. The Texans defending the north wall turned to meet the new threat and forgot that the Mexicans behind them were still trying to scale the walls. The Mexicans, realizing that this was their last opportunity, fought their way to the top.

Instantly, the Texans on the north wall were surrounded. Caught in the open, there was nothing they could do. Those who were able abandoned the wall. Those who were not died where they stood.

Hundreds of the enemy poured through the breach, led by a Mexican officer who saw the mortally wounded Alamo commander sitting on the ground. He thrust at his enemy with his sword but Travis was faster; parrying and lunging, he pushed his own sword through the Mexican. They fell and died together.

Defense in the north collapsed as the survivors abandoned their positions and the Mexicans poured over the wall. In the south, the defenders had fought the Mexicans to a standstill for the third time, but they soon had to give up. With their backs unguarded, they could do nothing but abandon the wall. The third assault had succeeded.

But the Alamo had not yet been taken. There were still about one-hundred defenders alive and continuing to fight.

Travis had planned ahead for the possible collapse of the walls. During the twelve days of siege, he and the men had spent time building barricades of dirt and stone in some of the barracks rooms. The earth parapets formed a semicircle around each door. They would offer the Texans a final protection, leaving the enemy vulnerable as he entered the barracks. But it was a last-ditch effort, one predestined to failure.

At the palisade defended by Davy Crockett, there never was an order to fall back. He and the Tennesseans were caught in the open as the Mexicans swarmed over the walls. The chapel was close, but still too far for them to reach. Surrounded, without a wall to put their backs against, they were quickly killed.

Crockett and two others were cut off on their way to the hospital. Standing back to back, they calmly loaded their rifles and fired into the Mexican infantrymen that were trying to reach them. Rifle balls dropped his two men, but Crockett held his ground. He seemed invulnerable.

Finally, a Mexican officer rushed up behind Crockett and swung his sword. The blow hit Crockett above the eye and he staggered. Before he could recover, a dozen bayonets pierced him and he fell.

With Crockett and his Tennesseans dead, there probably wasn't a defender left alive in the open with the exception of Jim Bonham and a small group who doggedly held the cannon on the chapel roof. They were working to turn one of the cannons so that they could fire it into the central plaza. With the Mexicans inside the Alamo, cannons pointing outside were useless.

They filled the barrel with scraps, stones, and anything else they could find, and fired, killing a dozen of the enemy and wounding many others. Those uninjured scrambled for hiding places and returned fire, trying to kill the artillerymen before they could touch off another shot.

As the Texans fired again, a hundred Mexican rifles opened up and each of the Texans fell.

From the windows and loopholes of the barracks came a steady stream of firing. In the main courtyard, the Mexicans were without cover. They tried to find some protection behind the bodies of the dead, but it wasn't enough and it wasn't easy. They had no choice but to attack the rooms.

The first to try died. They couldn't even get the doors open. But they quickly solved that problem. Turning the captured 18-pounder, they loaded it and fired, splintering a door. The infantry rushed in. Fighting was hand to hand, bayonet against Bowie knife. In seconds it was over, and the Mexicans turned to another room.

Finally the Alamo belonged to the Mexicans, except for the chapel and a few rooms on the south wall. Mexican infantry were breaking into the last of those rooms when they found Jim Bowie. Bowie killed the first two in with pistols given to him by Crockett, and then he killed two more with his knife, but it took all the strength he had. Mexican bayonets finished him.

Now all the defenders, except for a very few, were dead. The chapel was the only part of the Alamo that didn't belong to the Mexicans. Using the cannon that Crockett and his Tennesseans had fired from their palisade, the Mexicans were able to blast open the huge wooden doors of the chapel. They rushed in and the few defenders left could do very little.

Robert Evans had been detailed to blow up the powder magazine if the fort fell. Although badly wounded, he grabbed a torch and crawled forward. The Mexicans stopped him with a musket ball.

Quickly the Mexicans forced their way into all the rooms of the chapel. They killed the two young sons of one of the defenders but ignored 15-year-old Enrique Esparsa who was trying to hide.

Brigido Guerrero met the Mexicans with his hands up, shouting in Spanish that he had been a prisoner of the Texans. The Mexican soldiers believed him and let him go. He may have been the only defender to survive the final assault.

As Sue Dickinson watched, Jacob Walker ran into the room searching for a place to hide. A dozen Mexicans followed and bayoneted him. Outside she could still hear firing and didn't know that Walker was the last defender to die.

Moments later, a Mexican officer entered the chapel and called to her. At first she ignored him, but he said that it was the only way she could save both her life and the life of her daughter. She answered the officer, and he escorted her out of the chapel, through the fort littered with the bodies of men she had known, and then outside the Alamo. Behind her, all the firing had ended. By 6:30 AM, the Alamo had fallen, the defenders killed, and the only sound to be heard was a rumbling thunderstorm east of the fort.

Internal Letter

★TA★

FROM: Officer of the Corporate Historian

TO: President, Texas-American
Enterprises
Corporate Capital
New Dallas,
Denova

Sir:

In the process of reviewing the corporate records,
I uncovered the notes made by H. Perot Lewis and his
assistant, Michael Travis, concerning efforts to change the
natural course of history. I found that direct intervention was
needed to compensate for the interference by the band of
mercenary soldiers recruited by Lewis and the Texas-
American Oil Company.

There remains little doubt that the mercenaries
were successful in accomplishing their task of breaking the
Mexican siege of the old Franciscan mission popularly known
as the Alamo. The introduction of late Twentieth Century
weaponry on the side of the Texas rebels, produced inordinate
and sustained casualties among the Mexican forces, who
employed mass-assault tactics rather than the fundamental
principles of stealth, surprise, and fire and movement.

This dangerous precedent, accompanied by
Millsaps' suggestion to William Barret Travis (the Alamo
commander and a great-great-great-grandfather of Michael
Travis) that the remaining Mexican forces should be pursued
into Northern Mexico and crushed, was designed to permit
the future aquisition of vast oil fields in Mexico by Lewis.

Although there were a number of variables
operating in the plan, it was a success. A man of the cunning
and ruthless resourcefulness of Lewis, who had at his disposal

both a system for affecting trans-spacio-temporal travel and the financial resources to back it up, could succeed in his efforts to obtain any goal he set.

It would make little difference to the world, as a whole, that the Alamo fell in 1836. And, it would make little difference if Lewis had been successful in obtaining the oil fields in Mexico. What was important, however, was the interconnection of Lewis' plot, the fate of the Alamo, and the role played by time travel in the affair.

The situation, a single individual having the capability to rewrite history, is clearly unacceptable. Even with the mercenaries deciding, for whatever reason, to stay in the past, Lewis' plan would have succeeded and Lewis would then have been encouraged to attempt other changes.

During the last week, I have issued a series of memos outlining the history of the siege of the Alamo as it should have progressed. This data was gathered using the Tucker Transfer as well as the Hendrickson Interdimensional Guidance System, and a Series-9000 Historic Coordinator.

By analyzing all the data, I discovered that I could leave everything alone through March 5, 1836. The mercenaries, feeling that their job was done, withdrew from the Alamo and scattered throughout the United States and its territories. None of them caused any further problems. They lived quietly, building personal fortunes, but rather than influencing history, they profited from it.

I was able, using the disguise of a Mexican officer, to convince Santa Anna that the defense of the Alamo had been a lucky fluke, and that by seeming to withdraw and then returning with the majority of his army, he could take the fort. At first he was skeptical, but his hatred of the Texans, and the humiliation of the defeat made him overlook the questions that he should have been asking. He immediately called his officers together and issued the appropriate orders. I did find it necessary to use the Einstein Unified Matter Transmitter to move several thousand soldiers fifty miles closer to San Antonio. This was done without their knowledge and made less of an impact on history than trying to resurrect the men who had died in the earlier battle. I also made use of conventional environmental control technology to artificially induce a thunderstorm which masked the troop movements and covered the sound of the final battle, thereby

precluding the mercenaries from becoming aware of the
renewed attack and returning to interfere further.

    The attack came on March 6, one day later than
originally. Travis and the Texans were not overly surprised
and resisted for nearly two hours, but the Alamo fell, as
history demanded. As happens when one side is annihilated,
the rumors, half-truths, and legends come so mixed with fact,
that no one could really determine what had happened. It is
interesting to note that the names of all the mercenaries, as
well as the names of Dr. Tucker's assistants, who were
inadvertently taken back, appear on the lists of those who
died at the Alamo. This is probably the result of the final
messenger leaving the Alamo before Brown and his
mercenaries departed, and were believed, by him, to still be
present when the fort was taken.

    Since the mercenaries never returned, and
because the Alamo fell, and because Tucker could not solve the
problem of the death of returning time travelers, Lewis never
knew that his plan succeeded. Tucker, on the other hand, did.
He received a letter addressed to him and held in trust by a
San Antonio Law Firm. The only problem was that Tucker
never did find a way of safely bringing back people who had
stayed more than an hour in the past, and rather than kill his
assistants, he left them in 1836. He could have communicated
with them, following the instructions of the letter, but decided
that it would be kinder to let them believe that someday he
would come for them, rather than telling them that they were
stuck in the past forever.

    With this, history was put back on its original
path. Lewis died twelve weeks after the mercenaries were
dispatched and Michael Travis succeeded him to the
presidency of Texas-American. He was impeached several
months later when irregularities were found in the corporate
books. The new president put the corporation back on the
course it was meant to follow. Investigation by several
committees given authority by the old constitutional
government of the United States of America found the
corporation in violation of many laws, but none of the officers
guilty. The guilty had already been removed.

    Tucker was content to work on viewing the past.
The news of his invention eventually leaked and the
government took over regulation of it. Since there was the
problem of keeping people alive after a trip, no one made any

new attempts at time traveling. By the time a method was
discovered, the potential danger of changing history was so
firmly understood, that no one wanted to attempt to change
anything. They would observe and study, but they would never
again interfere.

If there are any further questions, please feel free
to contact me or any of my assistants. A full report,
containing an account of my intervention will be forwarded in
time for consideration by the Executive Council at the next
annual stockholders meeting.

Sincerely yours:

Halicar, HISTORIAN
First Assistant to the Chief Archivist

ATTACHMENT #1

The men who died at the Alamo.

Abamillo, Juan

Allen, R.

*Andross, M. J.

Autry, Micajah

Badillo, Juan A.

*Baily, Peter James

Baker, Isaac G.

Baker, William
    Charles M.

Ballentine, John J.

Ballentine, Richard W.

Baugh, John J.

Bayliss, Joseph

*Blair, John

*Blair, Samuel B.

Blazeby, William

Bonham, James Butler

Bourne, Daniel

Bowie, James

Bowman, Jesse B.

**Bromhead, Gronville

Brown, George

Brown, James

*Brown, Robert

Buchanan, James

Burns, Samuel E.

Butler, George D.

Campbell, Robert

*Cane, John

Carey, William R.

Clark, Charles Henry

*Clark, M.B.

Cloud, Daniel William

*Cochran, Robert E.

Cottle, George
    Washington

Courtman, Henry

*Crawford, Lemuel

Crockett, David

*Crossman, Robert

Cummings, David P.

*Cunningham, Robert

Darst, Jacob C.

Day, Freeman, H.K.

Day, Jerry C.

Daymon, Squire

*Dearduff, William

*Dennison, Stephen

Despallier, Charles

Dickinson, Almeron

Dillard, John H.

Dimpkins, James R.

Duel, Lewis
Duvalt, Andrew
Espalier, Carlos
Esparza, Gregorio
Evans, Robert
Evans, Samuel B.
Ewing, James L.
Fishbaugh, William
Flanders, John
Floyd, Dolphin Ward
*Forsyth, John Hubbard
Fuentes, Antonio
Fuqua, Galba
Furtleroy, William H.
**Garnett, William
Garrand, James W.
**Garrett, James Girand
Garvin, John E.
Gaston, John E.
George, James
Goodrich, John C.
Grimes, Albert Calvin
Gwynne, James C.
*Hannum, James
Harris, John
Harrison, Andrew
    Jackson
Harrison, William B.
**Hawkins, Joseph M.
Hays, John M.
Heiskell, Charles M.

Hendricks, Thomas
Herndon, Patrick H.
Hersee, William D.
Holland, Tapley
*Holloway, Samuel
Howell, William D.
Jackson, Daniel
*Jackson, Thomas
Jameson, Green B.
Jennings, Gordon C.
Johnson, Lewis
Johnson, William
Jones, John
Kellog, Johnnie
Kenny, James
*Kent, Andrew
Kerr, Joseph
*Kimball, George C.
King, William P.
Lewis, William Irvine
Lightfoot, William J.
Lindley, Jonathan L.
**Linn, William
Main, George W.
Malone, William T.
Marshall, William
Martan, Albert
McCafferty, Edward
McCoy, Jesse
McDowell, William
*McGee, James

McGregor, John

McKinney, Robert

Melton, Eliel

Miller, Thomas R.

Mills, William

*Millsaps, Isaac

Mitchusson, Edward

Mitchell, Edwin T.

Mitchell, Napoleon

Moore, Robert B.

**Moore, Willis

Musselman, Robert

Nava, Andres

Neggan, George

Nelson, Andrew M.

Nelson, Edward

Nelson, George

Northcross, James

Nowlin, James

Pagan, George

Parker, Christopher

Parks, William

Perry, Richardson

Pollard, Amos

Reynolds, John P.

Roberts, Thomas H.

Robertson, James

Robinson, Isaac

Rose, James M.

Rusk, Jackson J.

Rutherford, Joseph

Ryan, Isaac

Scurlock, Mial

*Sewell, Marcus L.

Shied, Manson

Simmons, Cleland K.

Smith, Andrew H.

Smith, Charles S.

Smith, Joshua G.

Smith, William H.

Starr, Richard

**Stewart, James E.

Stockton, Richard

Summerlin, A. Spain

*Summers, William E.

Sutherland, William D.

Taylor, Edward

Taylor, George

Taylor, James

Taylor, William

Thomas, B. Archer

Thomas, Henry

*Thompson, Jessie G.

Thomson, John W.

Thurston, John M.

Trammel, Burke

Travis, William Barret

Tumlinson, George W.

Walker, Asa

Walker, Jacob

Ward, William B.   Williamson, Hiram J.

Warnell, Henry   Wilson, David L.

Washington, Joseph G.   Wilson, John

*Waters, Thomas   **Wolfe, Antony

Wells, William   Wright, Claiborne

White, Isaac   Zanco, Charles

White, Robert

*Denotes Texas-American employee

**Denotes Texas-American employee killed in action

ATTACHMENT #2

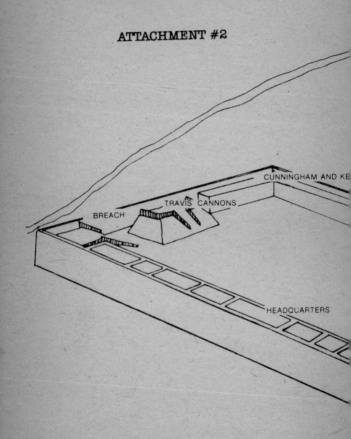

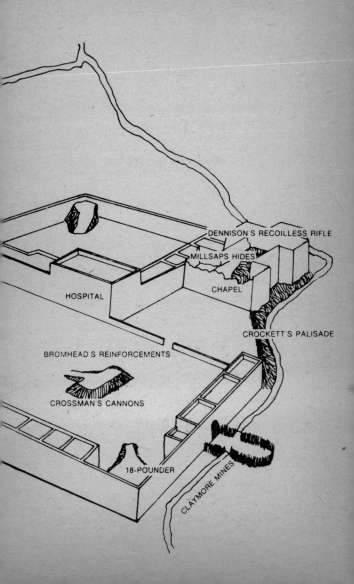

DENNISON'S RECOILLESS RIFLE

MILLSAPS HIDES

HOSPITAL

CHAPEL

CROCKETT'S PALISADE

BROMHEAD'S REINFORCEMENTS

CROSSMAN'S CANNONS

18-POUNDER

CLAYMORE MINES

ATTACHMENT #3

The following is a chronology of the Battle of the Alamo as it happened.

October 5, 1835	A formal declaration of war is published in Texas.
October 13, 1835	Mexicans in Gonzales, Texas, try to recover a cannon and find an "army" of 500 Texans.
October 28, 1835	Texans and Mexicans fight at Concepcion.
November 1, 1835	Texans surround General Cos, Santa Anna's brother-in-law in the Alamo.
November 28, 1835	Santa Anna leaves Mexico City with his army.
December 5, 1835	Texans launch attack on San Antonio.
December 9, 1835	Cos surrenders Alamo and leaves Texas.
December 30, 1835	James Grant leads 200 men out of San Antonio to attack Matamoros, Mexico.
January 17, 1836	James Bowie arrives at the Alamo.
February 3, 1836	William Travis arrives in San Antonio.

February 4, 1836	Alamo commander Joseph Neill leaves. Bowie and Travis organize a co-command.
February 11, 1836	Davy Crockett arrives.
February 15, 1836	Rumors sweep San Antonio that Santa Anna is near.
February 22, 1836	Alamo garrison throws a party for Crockett.
February 23, 1836	Townspeople rush to leave town.
February 23, 1836	Late in the afternoon, the first units of the Mexican army are spotted.
February 23, 1836	Travis responds to a surrender demand with a single cannon shot.
February 23, 1836	Mexicans raise a red flag in the Military Plaza.
February 23, 1836	Santa Anna arrives at the Alamo at sunset.
February 24, 1836	Bowie collapses and leaves Travis in sole command.
February 24, 1836	Albert Martin rides out with a message.
February 26, 1836	Fannin leaves Goliad on rescue attempt.
February 27, 1836	Fake attacks and bombardment continue.
February 28, 1836	Fannin returns to Goliad.

February 29, 1836	Bonham arrives in Goliad, gives his message to Fannin and then leaves.
March 1, 1836	Bonham arrives in Gonzales.
March 1, 1836	About midnight, 33 people enter the Alamo after fighting their way through the Mexican lines.
March 2, 1836	Rumor that Fannin is coming sweeps the Alamo.
March 3, 1836	Bonham returns with the news that Fannin isn't coming.
March 3, 1836	John W. Smith leaves with messages.
March 4, 1836	North wall is breached.
March 5, 1836	Attacks begin late in the day.
March 5, 1836	By 8:00 p.m., Santa Anna realizes that he has failed.
March 6, 1836	At 5:00 a.m. new assaults begin.
March 6, 1836	By 6:00 a.m. the final assault has started.
March 6, 1836	By 6:30 a.m. the battle is over.

Special note: Chronology may be off slightly. Records are not easy to find. The final attacks may have started as late as March 6, with no major fighting on March 5. Records do show that less than 12 hours passed from the beginning of the attacks to the fall of the Alamo. They also show that the final battle might have lasted less than three hours.